T0064273

(An Anecdote About Man Overboard.)

PARTRIDGE
A Penguin Random House Company

To order additional copies of this book, contact
Partridge India
000 800 10062 62
orders.india@partridgepublishing.com

www.partridgepublishing.com/india

For Maa and Paa.

I hope you're proud of me.

This book is fiction, and the characters are influenced by, but NOT based on real human beings. Nobody died, nobody cried, and nobody dug their noses.

Kill Your Heroes is my first creation that I've ever been proud of. I hope you like reading it, but there's a possibility that you might hate it, I'm not sure.

If you cry, or laugh, you're welcome.
No, sorry, that's kinda rude.

I mean, um, read on.

Yours truly,
Akshat Thakur

P.S. Happy ending!

My father always said, "Young man, it's alright to have a sore throat, as long as you don't have a sore brain."

I didn't get a drift of what he meant, until now.

Inspiration is obstreperous to find.

My name is Adam Timberlake.

I think I might be depressed.

The most depressing part of it is that I don't know why. There are a million things that make me anxious.

Loneliness would be the most prevalent form of war in my mind.

Even though I knew I had friends, I also knew that they wouldn't miss me after a day after my funeral. I wanted to die.

Not a painful death. No. No one wants to die painfully.

No one really wants to die. Everyone wants to go to heaven.

Yeah, no one wants to die. But I do. I really do.

Sometimes I feel like a ghost. A ghost walking amongst the living. I can't do this anymore.
I have to pee.

Ialwayspeeontheothersideofthetoilettomakelessnoise.

I flushed, after I was done. The water whooshed, like a world wind over my head, well, not over, but below my man-stuff. Like a whirlpool. I wish I were a microorganism that'd get flushed.

Unrequited love hurts. A rose left to die hurts. An unsent letter hurts. Being broken hurts. A worthless boy hurts.

Everything hurts.

The night was dark. It was a dark night. No. Not dark. Black. The night was black. Blacker than black. The blackness reflected off the dark side of the moon.

Tick, tick, tick.

Onomatopoeia is effective. The clock was ticking. Louder than it's mostly heard. It was almost like there was blood on the hands of the clock. There are things that we can, and things we cannot change.

I closed my eyes. The blackness was the same. I could hear my heart beat, almost as loud as I could feel it. The winds gushed. Into the night, I fell asleep.

JANUARY 19

It's Thursday, today. I wake up. I shower, steaming water. I wish I'd just turn into vapor, like these droplets would, if heated to a little more extent. I brush my teeth. I spill out the fluids inside my mouth, like I wish my guts would spill. I drink the glass of milk my mother had kept on my bedside table, at 6:30. I brush my teeth, again. I wear my dad's orange polo shirt, and my grey shorts. I pull up my socks. I put on my purple-black 'All-Star's. I dry my hair with the towel, and they return to their normal, messy self. I pack my bag, and put in all the books I'd need today. I say, 'bye' to my mother, and I leave the house. I leave the front door open. I walk down 14 fleets of stairs. The elevator isn't working, today. I wait for the bus to come.

I wait. I see the bus coming. If only it'd run me over. They my parents could sue the driver, or the school. If not, at least they'd inherit whatever my life is medically worth, from my medical insurance.

That's not enough payment for raising a shit-faced, disappointing excuse of a son, though.

The bus stops. I get on the bus.

After picking up some more, the bus goes towards the school. I wish that a black Chevrolet Impala would crash into the bus, right where I'm sitting.

But, no. I know that's never going to happen.

Extremely improbable to occur.

The bus stops. I get off. I walk past the school gates, and into the senior wing. I climb another three fleets of stairs. I meet my chum, Digboi Murray, on the way. Digboi is a fat person. He's extensively tanned, and has an emo haircut. His bangs don't suit him at all, but I never tell him that, because it's none of my business telling people what looks good on them and what doesn't.

D: "Hey, man."
A: "Hey."

I hear people whisper, as we pass them by. It doesn't bother me. People talk. They always do. They judge. They can't help but judge. They judge, like I breathe. We try not to, but we do, anyway.

I had friends, back in 7th grade. I was never much social anyway, but now that I'm totally cut off, I understand what a promising but flawed system 'life' is.

Digboi considers me as a friend, and don't get me wrong, he's amazing, but he's better off without me.

I go for my classes. I learn things that we are forced to, but I know that I'm never really going to use them in real life, anyway. Real life is a debatable topic. It's a relative term. Real life is good for certain people. For certain people, it's fine, not much struggling to live. Others' real life is a subsistence crisis. Then there are people who do not want life, at all.

"Hey, lad."

I heard from behind. I didn't even have to look, to know whom that smug voice belonged to. David Short. Such an ironic name. David Short is in fact, moderately tall.

I'm not very fond of jocks. David was the alpha jock. The stereotypical football team captain who dates the school's prettiest cheerleader? David's that guy.

I'm not very fond of jocks. Jocks aren't very fond of me.

Another key point, David holds an extreme grudge against me, ever since I asked out his girlfriend,

Selena Goldman. Of course, she said no, but David felt some kind of unprecedented danger, and he hates me for that.

"Hey, lad!"

I try to just walk past him. Ignorance is bliss, isn't it?

But some girls just ask for trouble.

Crap. I couldn't quite pull that one off.

"Hey, lad!"
…And he shoved me.

I have a well-balanced balancing mechanism, so I didn't fall. My ear fluids didn't fail me now. *Papa's proud of you.*

A: "What do you want, man?"
D: "I want my money, dawg."

David Short that he looks cool when he tries to act as a hackneyed convict.

A: "What money?"
D: "Uh… my pizza money!"
A: "What are you talking about?"
D: "Imma whip you, son!"
A: "Okay."
D: "Imma go Mike Tyson on yo' ass!"
A: "Do you even know who Mike Tyson is?"

D: "Yeah, dawg. He a wrestler, wee lad."
A: "Uh huh, sure."

If I had three ounces of confidence, I would seriously have punched the guy. Boxing is very precious to me, and if someone doesn't know who Mike Tyson is, he's certainly a stupid bozo.

Yet, calling Mike Tyson a wrestler is like mistaking Morgan Freeman for Nelson Mandela.

Morgan Freeman is cool. (I love his show, 'Through The Wormhole with Morgan Freeman'. It's pretty interesting.)

D: "What you lookin' at, son?"
A: "Nothing."
D: "Don't lie. I saw you lookin' at me, slick. What happened? My girl not hot enough fo' you?"
A: "No, seriously. I wasn't looking at you."
D: "Shut up, you lil' wee lad."

Again, I'm not very fond of jocks.

I wasn't even looking towards David.

His mother probably never gave him her attention when he was a baby.

Stupid attention-seeking, attention deficit bozo.

I just walked away from there, before he alleged me of any more homosexual acts.

"Bro, this guy was lookin' at my man goodness."

I crash into Digboi.

Digboi. Wait. It just hit me. His name is hilarious. Why would any parent do that their child?

I crash into ~~*beep*boy~~ Digboi.

A: "Sorry, man."
D: "It's okay."
A: "So, where are you going?"
D: "Mrs. K. Coming with me?"
A: "Sure."

I followed Digboi, and we looked for Mrs. K.

Mrs. K. taught chemistry. She was a good teacher, with a peculiar sense of humor.

Mrs. K.: So, a beggar was sitting outside MIT… a student went to him and asked him, "What's the matter with you?"

Class (in unison): What did the beggar say?

Mrs. K.: The beggar said, "Gas, liquid, solid, plasma, Einstein-Bose condensate".

Digboi found Mrs. K., drinking coffee. I waited for him, while he talked to her.

"Good morning, ma'am."
"Good afternoon, Dig."
"Here's my homework."
"Good boi."
"Thank you."

He handed his assignment over to Mrs. K., and we walked away. We just kept walking, like the winds blow over the mountains, oh, so cold.

A: "When are we going to record our album?"
D: "I don't know."
A: "Digboi, tell me!"
D: "I don't know."
A: "Come over on Sunday."
D: "Okay."

Digboi and I have a band. Well, there is only the two of us, so it's technically a duo. But, whatever. I play the rhythm and bass guitars, and I sing, and Digboi plays piano and also the guitar. I've written 15 songs, but we haven't recorded anything, yet. The band is called 'Eternal Subside'. Don't ever leave me with a thesaurus.

I don't really know how to play the guitar, so I just keep playing the A, D, Em, and power chords, with a bit of palm muting. Digboi, however, is an amazing pianist. He'll probably pursue a diploma. We try to sound like a punk-rock band, and the both of us know that we need a talented drummer for that, and neither one of us wants to admit that we suck.

"People haven't always been there for me but music always has."
—Taylor Swift

Music is the most eloquent form of communication I can muster. As if the lyrics are straight up directed towards me, Punk Rock is the most enchanting form of chords, vocals, beats, and breathtaking lyrics, put together by strings of magic.

It makes severely depressed people feel better, like there is still a tiny rope of hope. A sense of being wonder-struck is achieved, straight inside the heart.

It was lunchtime, soon.

I just remembered some words that compliment each other.

Always, I know you'll be at my show,
Watching, waiting,

Commiserating.

I looked up at the ceiling, If only it fell. Right on me.

What if the sky fell down?

I know it's practically impossible for the sky to fall down.

You're getting more stupid every day, man.

I know. I'm sorry.

Yeah, you better be. You know how much we hate stupid bozos.

My heart's all gone. I can feel it.

No, I cannot feel it. That's how I know it's gone.

Holy crap! If your heart were gone, you'd be dead.
Yeah, I know.
Good.

I wish my heart really were gone. And so were I.

I wish I could fly.

How can I fly, when they keep cutting off my wings?

Someday soon. Someday, I'll fly.

I clenched my fists, and I looked at myself, in the mirror. A sudden burst of extreme disenchantment overtook me. I couldn't even look anymore. Wretchedness clouded my eyes. I turned back, and I ran my fists into the wall. I kept striking, and striking. I heard my knuckles crumble, and I knew I would stumble, but I couldn't stop.

When pain killed my honor, I fell to the ground. I hate myself.

~~I hate myself.~~
~~I hate myself.~~
~~I hate myself.~~
I ~~h~~ate myself.
~~I hate myself.~~
I hate myself.

I came out of the boy's washroom. I went to the lockers, to get my books for Algebra II. What's my passcode again? 0109. I looked for my books, and pen. History, no. Chemistry, no. Physics, no. Algebra, yes. There you are.

I picked up the books, and I gazed upon a small piece of parchment. I thought it'd just be lyrics of some All Time Low song, sneaked into my locker by Sidnee, one of my best friends. She took almost all the classes I did.

Like always, I thought wrong. But I wouldn't know that. And I was running out of time. So, I just folded the papyrus, and put it in my pocket.

Algebra passed like a tidal wave. So did the rest of the day. My thoughts, crumpled, like the eternal note, deep in my pocket.

—————————————————————————

S: "Hey."
A: "Hi."
S: "What's going on?"
A: "Nothing much. What about you?"
S: "Just looking forward to go home."
A: "Yeah."
S: "So, how are you, Adam?"
A: "I'm fine."

~~Anything but fine.~~
~~Anything but fine.~~
~~Anything but fine.~~
~~Anything but~~ fine.

A: "I'm fine. How are you?"
S: "I'm great! Thea's sister got us tickets to A Day To Remember!"
A: "That's so cool. So cool."
S: "I know! So cool!"
A: "So, when is it?"
S: "Saturday… oh, do you want to come?"
A: "No, you know how I hate crowds."
S: "You don't hate crowds. You just fear them. You're afraid of crowds."

Sidnee knows me like the back of her hand. That's what she thinks, and what I like to believe, anyway. I wish I could tell her everything. But if I did, she would either hate me, or think that I'm a psycho-depressed-attention-seeking-maniac. She probably already does.

Well, you are a psycho-depressed-attention-seeking-maniac.
Yeah, I know.
Good.
Do you want a sucker punch to your face?
You can't kill your inner-inner voice.
Yeah, I know.
Stupid bozo.

I've never told Sidnee that I have an inner-inner voice that talks to my inner voice. I've never told Sidnee how lonely I feel.

I've never told anyone.
I'm a train wreck. No, I'm the paroxysm that wrecks the train.

I'm a walking travesty.

I hate everything. I hate myself. If only I was terminally ill.

Misery loves company, but I do not. Sometimes, I feel like loneliness is tearing me apart, but I'm the only one to blame for it all. I just cannot let someone in.

When I look at the stars, I don't see them shine. I look at the future, a billion years in, when all the stars become black holes.

Black holes always remind me of dark places. Dark, like my thoughts. My thoughts all turn to ash. And my conscience burns me, inside.

We stopped looking for monsters under our beds, when we realised they were inside us.

My monsters still haunt me. They don't let me sleep. They don't let me smile. They don't let me cry. They don't let me live. They don't let me die.

They make my head hurt. They make me wonder why.

The worst part of not being able to cry is that you can't let your feelings out. I feel jealous of babies, who cry for petty reasons, like: 'Hey, ma, gimme milk!' 'I've got a Christmas gift for you, it's in my diaper.' 'This guy scares the crap out of me. Literally.' 'Wipe my butt, yo.'

~~~~~~

I board the bus. The bus is about to leave, when Sally nippily boards it.

Sally is kind of pretty. She's short. She must be 5'4". She has curly brown hair, and dark brown eyes. Her curves are nice. She's wearing a black sweater. She's a dazzling dancer. She's got a perennial smile. It's nice.

S: "Scoot over."
A: "Okay."
I move, and she sits beside me.
A silence follows.
S: "Adam, I talked to Selena. She says that she would date you if you were her age. Dude. I mean wut? Why do you like senior girls? She's like… 2 years older than you."
A: "Oh, my god, stop. Stop, Sally. I don't even like her."

S: "Yeah, right. That's wut you said about Robin."

Robin Chuckles was my first crush. I started developing a liking for her in fifth grade. We were pretty inordinate friends, back then. I didn't stop liking her, though. Finally, in the eighth grade, when I accumulated all the courage I could, I asked her out. She, indirectly, said no; through a maybe. *Maybe.* I hate that word. I asked her out, about thrice more, and she delicately rejected me. Very delicately, indeed. I haven't seen her since her 15th birthday. I think she only called me to her party because she felt guilty about saying no to me, and/or pitied me.

A: "Fine. But seriously. I just think that she's really pretty."
S: "Yeah, I know. See, you like Selena."
A: "I used to like her. I asked her out, too. She's dating David, anyway."
S: "Aww, I know."
Everyone is always talking about their girlfriends, and boyfriends, and kissing; and I'm here, alone, writing a thesis on a theory I can't possibly prove.

After a while of silence, I hear Ronnie, a sixth grader say,
"Dude, let me excrete in peace."

After about 30 seconds, I start laughing. I can't stop laughing. I wonder if some has pumped up some Nitrogen. Sally looks at me.

S: "What the heck, Adam?"

A: "He... he said... he said... excrete."

I choke. I'm choking on my own laughter. I cannot breathe. If I die now, it'd be the best way to die. Let me excrete in peace.

This could be my epiphany.

Sally asks the sixth grader what he said. She starts laughing. Her laugh is slightly irritating, but incredible, too. She says, croaking:

"Hehehe. Funny."

The bus drops Sally off. The bus drops me off. The elevator has been fixed. Even with all the perks of gravity, I highly disregard it. It makes climbing the stairs an incredibly hard undertaking.

I'm inside the elevator. I press '7'. A probable seventeen year old walks in, just as the doors of the winch-like elevator close. This odd looking male, with a particularly big nose, takes the position near the scratched mirror of the elevator. I try not to stare, while he tries not to dig his nose. I do, anyway, and he does, too.

I wish I hadn't seen him putting that relatively large piece of snot in his mouth, and rather enjoying the splendid taste of mucus and cilia.

I shrug, as soon as he gets off, at the sixth floor. I get off, at the seventh. I walk 15 steps, to the right, and look at the gold-plated digits, 713. The 7 is slightly tilted, the 1 and 3 are perfectly placed. I ring the doorbell. My mother lets me in.

She received a call from another client, so she didn't ask me the typical 'how was school?' question. I went to my room, and I lay on my bed, with nothing going on inside my head.

Oh my god. Of course something's going on inside your head, bozo! All your body processes are supervised by your brain.
Yeah, I know. That was just a phrase.
Shut up. You're stupid.
I know.
You should get all your shit together.
I've really got to get my shit together.
Yeah, bozo. You should improve your grades. Those Bs aren't fooling anyone. You won't get into a good college, if you don't. And you know how bad you want to get into MIT.
I'm aware of that.
I know you are. Do something about it.
I just can't get rid of all these problems.
Shut up, and do something about it.
I can't fix this. But I need to.

I closed my eyes, to escape my fate for a little while. I ran my hands through my jeans, and a folded piece of paper fell through my pocket.

Hi, Adam.
I'm in love with you. You're amazing. Never change, okay?
-Anonymous

I read it thrice. It was written so beautifully. It couldn't be a hoax, as Sidnee has a good handwriting, but she wouldn't really pull off this kind of a practical joke.

It must be some guy messing with you.
I know.
Yeah.
Yeah.
But what if it's some really hot chick?
That'd be cool.
Yeah, it would.

I picked up my basketball, and put on my earphones. I left the house, with my iPod thumping in my ears.

I went to the nearby basketball court. No one ever comes here. I'm usually the only one playing.

I just run around, chasing the ball, like a dog, as it deflects, every time I miss a shot.

I'd never thought that I'd be like this. So alone and lost.

If people were ships, I'd be the Titanic.

I'm the killer wave of the beach.
Heaven is way out of my reach.

I go back home, study for my History test,
tomorrow; my mom gives me dinner; I say good
night to my dad and mom; and I sleep.

I can't dream anymore.

It's Friday, today. Rebecca Black's very infamous song comes into mind, doesn't it? Anyway, it's Friday, today. I wish an angel dropped like an earthquake. NO. TOO MUCH DUBSTEP ON THE RADIO. I wish an angel fell from heaven, and saved me. But the only angels here are made of neon.

I take a shower. The water comes out, and the moment it touches my skin, I lose my mind.

Shit. Crap. This is cold!

Maybe the geyser wasn't working, today, either. I just stood under the shower, stuttering like crazy, my balls semi-frozen, teeth cluttering to the cold. After the shower, I grab a towel, and dry myself off. I wear my clothes, and I look myself in the mirror.

You. Yes, you, look at me.
I'm looking at you.
Good. You're stupid.
I know.
Good. You look like a bozo, today.
I know.
Everybody's going to make fun of you, in their minds, of course.
I know. They're all fake.

Not fake. They are plastic.
Not plastic. They are paper.

·····

I get on the bus, once again. Sally almost misses it, again. Ronnie cracks lame, but seriously hilarious jokes, and I almost choke on my laughter, again.

A: "What did Hitler say to the waiter?"

R: "What, Ronnie?"

A: "I want Apple Jews."

If I were a director, I would make Ronnie my male lead. I should probably tell him to stop with the unorthodox jokes, though.

Ronnie Summers is actually extremely smart. He's smarter than everyone else his age. He knows about the current affairs, and his knowledge about… everything, in general is pretty unsullied. And he looks up to me, for some reason, so I like him even more.

I high-five Ronnie, as we walk across the school gates, and he says,

"Goodbye, ma man."

"Bye, Ronnie."

·····

Last week, we had to memorize dialogues from Julius Caesar, as an English literature assignment. Fortunately, our teacher, Ms. Liliana Essient is very lenient towards everything, and she changed it to a book review on any book we wanted. I chose to do it on 'It's Kind of a Funny Story', by Ned Vizzini. While researching about Vizzini, I learned something extremely sad.

The world is crazy. So crazy that the word is too short a word to express the meaning.
Craziness rubs off the cold shadows of the world, onto the people we admire the most.
Peer pressure. Depression. Insecurities. Thank you so much, but no. Not anymore. Heck no.
Ned Vizzini, my favorite author, wrote about these subtleties so beautifully, that it would make melancholy turn into happiness. He committed suicide on January 17, 2013.

I was rooting for Craig, the protagonist of 'It's Kind of a Funny Story' to lose his depression, and survive. Hell, I was rooting for everyone else in his shoes, including myself. I was rooting for Ned Vizzini.

He was contemplating, ending himself for the best. It's pretty amazing that a person that was in such a dark place could hold on for so long. I mean, you would have thought he'd be contented with the 'good life', but nothing could hide his true emotions. A person can only contain himself for so long.

I can't hold on any longer.

I left a note inside my locker, for (probably a guy messing with me) my secret admirer.

Hey.
Thanks. However, I think I don't have a choice.
Please tell me who you are.

Yours Truly,
Adam.

Sometimes, I think I'll die alone. Think of it, no. I think of it all the time. Misery chokes me up. I wish I could get rid of it, but Misery is never going to stop exasperating me.

As for my insides, I'm sure they'll not rot when I'm dead, but scatter its atoms, as they break down further, all over the earth. It feels good to know that a part of me is the same of Einstein's.
I just cannot be an optimistic, though. I cannot be an optimistic about anything.

I am *atelophobic*.

Atelophobia; the fear of not being good enough.

I can't keep holding on, to nothing.
I give up.

Whenever I feel depressed, I eat donuts. It sounds crazy, but it helps. I dope on sugar, and that magically removes all the Prolactin from my body, and fills it with Endorphins. However, it makes me incredibly hyperactive. Part of why I don't have many friends is because I'm always high on Donuts, and I act weird most of the time.

The greatest thing about Donuts is that they heal me in a way that I never really needed to take Anti-depression or anti-anxiety pills.

I hate myself, but I love Donuts.

The bell rang, and I ran towards the class. I took my seat, as Mrs. Nicole passed the test papers. I looked around. I didn't find the hand of Death on my shoulder, which was sad. I looked at the questions.

Easy as can be.
Shut up. Over-confidence might get you a B.
Yeah, I know.
Good. You need to get an A. Understood?
Yes.

I kept writing, and writing, and writing. I could go on, forever. My handwriting is horrible, so I left a note, after I attempted the last question.

Dear Mrs. Nicole,
I'm sorry for the terrible handwriting. You see, I do not write
well, under pressure.
Yours Truly,
Adam T.

―――――――――――――――――――――――――――

"How'd your History test go?"
"Very well."
"That's nice. I'm proud of you, Adam."

You'd think this is an excerpt from a conversation with my mom. But no. Not really.

This was the conversation I had with Sidnee, during lunch break.

S: "What all tests do you have next week?"
A: "Economics, Civics, Geography. What about you?"
S: "I don't have any."
A: "That's cool."
S: "I know, right? So cool!"
A: "Man, I have Literature, next to next week, and Algebra and Geometry and Calculus, the week after the next to next week."
S: "Yeah. Lots to study."
A: "Yeah."
S: "I'm so excited."
A: "Why?"

S: (while jumping, and smiling excessively) "I'm going to see A.D.T.R, live!"

A: "Haha. I'm happy for you. Have fun!"

S: "You should come, too."

A: (looking down, and then shaking head) "Nah, I'll be fine. You guys have fun."

S: "Try not to kill yourself, okay?"

I rolled my eyes, then chuckled.

A: "Okay. Give my love to Thea. I'll just chill with ma boy Digboi."

S: "Sure. Sometimes, I swear that you seem more gay than Digboi."

I started staring into the nothing, again. I thought for a while, and then…

A: "Sidnee, I might be gay."

I wasn't even kidding. I hadn't really thought about it before. I did find guys like Alex Gaskarth and Michael Cera cute.

S: "What?"

A: "I might be gay."

S: "You're kidding me."

A: "No."

S: "Don't you like, like girls?"

A: "I do. I mean, I don't know."

S: "What do you mean?"

A: "I don't really fancy dating, anyway. It's just a waste of time."

S: "Uh, huh."

A: "I'm not going to get a girlfriend until I graduate from MIT, and get a job."

S: "You've got it all figured out, don't you?"

Sidnee often told me that she wished she had it all figured out, like me. She doesn't need to have it all figured out. She had a perfect 4.0 GPA, and she was in the Debate club, so she could get into any college she wanted.

S: "Anyway, Digboi isn't gay. Is he?"

A: "I know. He isn't."

S: "So, what's new?"

A: "Um, nothing. What about you?"

S: "C'mon Adam, something must be new."

A: "Well, I have a secret admirer."

S: "Oho. Do you know who it is?"

The whole concept of having a secret admirer is not knowing who it is. But whatever.

A: "No, I do not."

S: "Did she do anything to let you know she admires you?"

A: "She leaves notes in my locker."

S: "Uh, huh. That's cool."

I was feeling low, again, so I munched on a strawberry jelly-filled Donut.

There's so much that the future promises. The future is so promising.

I can't help but think what it'll be like. I look forward to the future so much, that I'm often neglecting the past.

~~~~~~

Every time my uncle comes over from some town near Canada, or we go to visit him, my dad and him drink plenty of whiskey. Whilst drunk, they have some very interesting tête-à-têtes. Their chats often end up with me getting a lecture about life. The last time we went to meet him, he said,
"Forget the past. Enjoy the present. Think about the future, but don't let it diminish your today."

He's pretty wise.

~~~~~~

I was sitting in Economics, writing a hook, when Mrs. Arianna asked us a question,
"What's the definition of poverty?"

I raised my hand, and said,
"The state of being poor. The situation a person gets into, when he cannot sustain his family."
"Good."

Henderson Gill shouts out,

"Obama lived in poverty till he was elected as
  President!"
Everybody knew that the fact was wrong, but chose
to ignore him.

Henderson shouts out, again,
  "My name Jeff!"
I just shook my head, and so did Mrs. Arianna.

I muttered,
  "And I wish I was deaf."

And whoever heard that, laughed.

Biology is sheer torture. I think that our teacher
has anger issues. She really needs Anger
Management. Not from Charlie Sheen, though.
Maybe it's a marriage gone bad, I'm not sure.

She reads out notes faster than a bullet train, and
expects us to write down everything, word-by-
word.

Biology is unbearable.

I don't even know why I took it in the first place. I
just took everything I thought would benefit me in
the long run.

I don't even score as well as I hoped I would. That
brings my entire average score down. My dad just
shakes his head whenever I tell him my actual
scores. I'm not into sports either, so as he calls it,

I'm the exact opposite of how he was, as a teenager.

He told me not to take all APs, and that I couldn't handle them. I just wanted to make him proud, so I did. And it backfired on me.
I'm just not good enough for him. I know that. And so does he. And it seriously hurts me to see how much I disappoint him.

I returned to get my books, for Physics. I opened my locker, and an apple fell out. And no, it didn't bounce off my feet, and I didn't catch it. I picked up the apple, from the ground, and a note was attached.

Hi, Adam.
I noticed you didn't eat anything but a doughnut during lunch. Here's an apple for you. (An apple a day keeps the doctor away.)
I can't tell you who I am. I am anonymous.
Your anonymous.
XOXO

I read it, and folded it, and kept it in my locker. I grabbed my books, and left.

How did she know about the Donut?
I don't know.
She's a stalker.

31

Maybe.
Probably.
Probably.

~~~~~~

I don't know why I was thinking about it, but I suddenly started thinking about this guy I read about.

So, Ronnie told me about this guy called Bob "Bobby" Dick doesn't have any legs. Yes, his parents did hate him. His dad wants him to compete in the Olympic games. And no, not in the Paralympics. So, his mother applied the right kind of pressure on him, and he started running like a normal son.

However that works.

~~~~~~

I felt like a thrashed mirror, broken into a million pieces. And the worst part of it all was that I was so down, for no reason at all. How pathetic is that?

I called 1-800-SUICIDE a while ago, and told them that I was depressed. The person on the line, who insisted me to call him 'Jeremiah Bro', asked me,

"Hello, Adam. Are you physically or sexually abused?"

Uh, no. If I did, I would have a reason to be sad.
"No."
"Are you dealing with loss of a loved one?"
"No."
"Have you done something terrible?"
"What do you mean?"
"Killed someone, or hurt someone?"
"No."
"Did your girlfriend cheat on you?"
"No, no."
"Oh, you sound gay. Boyfriend?"
"No, I'm not gay."
"You sure?"
"Yes.
"There's nothing wrong with being gay."
"I know."
"Cool, bro."
"Yeah."
"So, why the hell are you depressed?"
I wished I knew that. I just hung up on Jeremiah Bro, and ended up being more depressed than I originally was.

After Physics, I bumped into Thea.

Thea Mosley was pretty intimidating. And intimidatingly pretty. She absolutely loved punk rock, just as I did. She got furious if someone got even a little bit of her favorite songs wrong.

~~Last Christmas, I gave you my heart. But the very next day, you gave it away.~~ NO. WHAT THE *beep* AM I DOING?

On the day before Christmas, our school had a carnival. I normally wouldn't even have turned up, because the only thing I hate more than socialising is socialising at lame school events. Still, it was mandatory to come, as my club had a stall that I had to manage. Some lame ska bands were playing there. It was terrible.

A band with seven middle schoolers for vocalists performed 'SING' by My Chemical Romance. God-awful. I wanted to freaking strangle all of them.

I looked around, in hope of finding something that would distract me enough, to make me forget about this terrible ska band. I saw Thea, with the exact same face as mine. She hated that band for wrecking SING. I wanted to give her a hug, but I controlled my urges to do that.

Another band with a very dreadful singer performed 'Know Your Enemy' by Green Day, which was covered god-awfully, too. I was ready to leave, because, frankly, this shit made me sad. I called my dad to come pick me up, and I left in 15 minutes.

Well, the terrible ska bands weren't the only reason why I left. Sidnee ditched me to go 'hang out' with some of her 'other cooler friends', and I hate to admit it, but I felt minuscule loneliness.

I like Thea's hair.

"What are you doing, Adam?"
Oh, *beep*. I didn't realize I was fondling Thea's incredible, moderately curly hair.
    A: "Sorry."
    T: "It's okay, haha."
Thea's laugh was really cute.

If I told all this to Sidnee, she would probably want me to ask Thea out, or, not, because both of us know that I'm not her type.
    T: "Are you coming for A.D.T.R.?"
    A: "Um, no, I'm not."
    T: "Why? I thought you liked them."
    A: "I do. I just don't like crowds."
    T: "Oh yeah, Sidnee told me about your phobia."

Should I ask Thea out?
She'll say no, man.
Yeah. That's what I thought.
Yeah. Think of it this way. You'll not be wasting any time, like all those other ridiculous guys who keep dating chicks.
Yeah. That's pretty cool.
Yep. And we can't even be sure if Thea will make you happy.

You're right.
I always am.

Thea told me that she had some work to do, so I said bye to her.

I kept my books back in my locker, and I set off to find Digboi. Once I did, I told him that I figured out some wicked riffs, and he told me to make him hear those some time. We walked together, to find Sidnee. She was with Thea, 'fan-girling' about All Time Low's new album.

"I'll see you guys, later. I have some stuff to do."

I waved, and I went to the bathroom. No, I didn't really have 'some stuff to do'. I was just anxious again.

I can't blame it on the schooling system. Or anything else. The only thing I CAN blame is myself.

My life isn't bad. I have friends ~~(who probably hate me)~~. I have caring parents ~~(who I severely disappoint)~~. I have a secret admirer ~~(who is probably a guy pulling off a prank)~~.

I'm the only thing that's bad.

I looked at the mirror, and punched it, hard.

You can't kill me; no matter how hard you try.

I feel like I keep coming back to this. I would say Déjà vu, but it's a very mainstream expression, now (I would have said 'cliché', but 'cliché' is nothing but another 'cliché'.)

I'm running in circles, and I can't find myself.

I bashed my head into the wall, twice, and came out of the bathroom. I walked past David, who kept yelling,
"You my beyotch, beyotch."
...for some reason. And it was probably directed towards me. I observed Selena approach him, and yeah, they smooched. I tried not to see that nauseating scene, as I walked by.

Somebody was trying to slip something inside somebody else's locker. Wait. That looked like my locker.

Yes, it definitely was my locker.

I accelerated towards my locker, but couldn't quite catch up to that distant 'somebody'.

I found another note.

Hi, love.
I love you, you amazing boy. I want to talk to you. I love
talking.
-Anonymous.

I flipped it over, and wrote,

Hi.
You can talk to me anytime you want to.
Just tell me your name.

Well, at least she/he/it doesn't hate me. She/he/it
probably will, if she/he/it knew me, though.

━━━━━━━━━━━━━━━━━━━━━━━━━━━━━━━━

I sat in the bus, again, and Sally asked me to scoot
over, again, and fortunately, she didn't talk about
Robin or Selena, today.

We didn't even talk. It was awfully silent, until
Ronnie started singing a spoof-like version of
'Boulevard of Broken Dreams'.
"So, when I'm on the toilet,
I'm the only one, and I crap alone.
Uhuh, uhuh. I crap alone, I crap alone."

I got off the bus, as it dropped me off, and I went
home. I ate a sandwich my mom had made for me.
I cranked up some MTV, but they played One

Direction's new song, and that was terrible. So, I shut off the TV.

I put on my earphones, and I turned the volume loud.

She's unstoppable, so unpredictable,
I'm so jaded, calculated wrong.

I felt my phone vibrate.

It must be Digboi.
Or Sidnee.
Right, oh.
Let's just see.
Okay.

I picked up the phone off the table. It lay on my rough sketches of how a wormhole could look like.

I didn't see whom the call was from, just straight away picked it up.
"Hi."

And I knew.

 A: "Uh… hello."
 R: "Hi."
 A: "Hi."
 R: "Say something, please."
 A: "How have you been?"
 R: "I've been fine, Adam. How about you?"
 A: "Yeah, me too, Robin. How are you?"

R: "Umm…"

I felt something burn, at the back of my mind.

A million painful memories just scorching their way through, again.

R: "… I'm okay."
A: "Are you sure? You sound upset."
R: "How do you know?"
A: "I know you, Robin."
R: "I'm so happy that you do."
A: "Yeah…"
R: "How are you?
A: "I'm okay."
R: "Oh, okay. No. Wait. Are you depressed?"
A: "…"
R: "Say something, please."
A: "Never mind that."
R: "Please don't hang up on me."

I didn't say anything for a while, and then I said,
A: "I won't."
R: "Thank you so much."
A: "…Why are you calling me?"
R: "I just needed someone to talk to."
A: "Oh, okay."
R: "…"
A: "…"

The silence was killing me.

I shouldn't have asked her, but I did, anyway,

A: "Are you feeling alone, or lost?"

R: "..."

A: "It's okay, Robin, I feel it, too. I feel so disillusioned."

R: "...I..."

A: "I miss you."

R: "I miss you, too."

A: "..."

R: "..."

A: "Remember when I said I loved you? I meant it."

R: "I did, too. I love you, too, Adam."

A: "It just hurts. I know you're lying."

R: "I'm..."

A: "I'm sorry, Robin. I'm sorry for everything."

My mom called me, and I told Robin that I had to go.

It did hurt. So much.

I helped my mom out with a few things. She asked me how school was, and I told her that it was fine.

I went back to my room.
I felt so miserable. So lost.

Donuts?
No, you don't deserve Donuts.
I don't deserve anything.

I was done, just musing.

~~~~~~

I locked myself into my room. I put on Dance Gavin Dance on full volume, and started penning another song.

[CHORUS:]
Look up to the skies
Don't you close your eyes
Tell me what you see
These pigs can fly.
* INTRO *
[VERSE:]
She said she doesn't like my face
I gave her a kiss, she gave me mace
She said she hates the way I play the bass
I gave her a hug; she tossed me in the fireplace.

I kneeled on my knee, and pulled out a ring
She cut off my balls, I couldn't stop screaming
She said she hates the way I sing
I told her she keeps my heart from breaking.

I told her she gives me a state of grace
She said she needs some space
I offered her a rocket trip, she spit on my face
And she asked me this, 'fore she trashed my place.

[PRE-CHORUS:]

What's the meaning of life?
What's the meaning of life?
I hate your face
Can pigs fly?

[CHORUS:]
Look up to the skies
Don't you close your eyes
Tell me what you see
These pigs can fly.
x3

This turned out well. I never thought I would get inspired enough to write something like this.

I texted it to Digboi, and waited for his approval. But all he said was 'cool', which was good enough.

Things are actually going well.
What do you mean?
I'm acing my tests. I'm a bit inspired, even. I think I just might be happy.
I'm happy for you.

I finished my math homework, as well as my French assignment (thanks to Google Translate).

My phone vibrated inside my pocket.

A: "Yellow?"

S: "Hello."

A: "Orange?"

S: "Hi."

I could feel Sidnee laugh in her mind. She laughs at my lame jokes.

A: "Red?"

S: "Stop it, Adam."

A: "Purple?"

S: "No. Just no."

A: "Sorry, Sidnee."

S: "It's okay. What's up?"

A: "Homework. What about you?"

S: "Same here."

A: "So, how are you?"

S: "I'm great. How are you?"

A: "I'm better. I don't feel so empty anymore."

S: "How come? I mean, yay, good for you! But, how come?"

A: "Things are going pretty well."

S: "I'm so glad."

A: "I just have some things I need to figure out."

S: "Huh. Like what? I might be able to help."

I thought hard about what I was going to say. I kept thinking for about thirty seconds. Then, Sidnee heard me speak.

A: "I talked to Robin. She called me."

S: "Oh! How'd it go?"

A: "I just told her everything I felt, uh, in my heart."

S: "Uh, huh. Okay. So, what are you trying to figure out?"

A: "I think I still love Robin."

S: "What?"
A: "I've been battling this for so long. It's probably nothing, but I think I might love Robin."

Shit. Crap. I'm so confused. I'm so jaded.

Sidnee didn't reply for a while.
S: "Robin, that's obvious. You like her for what… 2 years?"
A: "I don't know. Maybe four. Maybe six."
S: "Wow. Six? Wow. But, yeah, it's Robin."
A: "Well, it's probably no one. I'm just too confused."

Neither one of us spoke, for about thirty seconds.

Then, I started making weird sounds, and I could hear Sidnee smile.

We talked for a while, and then we said goodbye.

I did my Literature homework. We had to write character sketches for the characters in the play Julius Caesar. It was very, very easy.

I went to the kitchen, to look for donuts, but couldn't find any. Shit. I could feel desolation bubble up, inside me.

I often wonder what makes us human. Is it merely the evolution, for the survival? Or is it more than that? I don't think we can fix everything. We just try. Bit by bit. We can just try to fix our lives. We could fix everything. But then, we would cease to exist.

I can't fix it, if I'm part of the problem.
Unless you cease to exist.
I wish that were an option.
It is. The question is, are you brave enough for it? Are you cowardly enough for it? Is it worth it? Answer these, and you'll know what the answer is.

The thing I hate the most is not being able to do what I want. Not being able to do what I desire.

I contemplate so much, but I can never actually go ahead with killing myself.

People often tell me that I can fix everything, if I learn how to eliminate these 'negative' thoughts.

If they only knew that these thoughts define me.

On better days, I hear Ronnie say,
"Oh, my butt!"
Or,
"The driver is stupid! Stupid crackpot!"
Or,
"Lick my crack, Jack!"
Or,
"You belong in Africa. What are you doing here?"
Or,
"You've got as many balls as Lindsay Lohan!
That's right. You got none at all!"
Or,
"Shit, shit, shittidy, shit. It's brown, and stinky, and
yummy to eat. Yeah, shit, shit, shittidy, shit. Your
momma will give you shit for Christmas."
Or,
"All hail Ronnie; kiss my ass."

I studied for my tests.

It was really easy to do numerical questions on the
Mole concept. I just wished we had more
interesting things in our syllabus, such as Quantum
Mechanics.

The only reason I want to get into MIT so bad is
because I'm absolutely in love with theoretical
physics. I saw my first Stephen Hawking lecture
when I was twelve, and I've wanted to be that

smart ever since. If I don't get into MIT, for obvious reasons like,

1. I don't have a 4.0 GPA.
2. I'm not in band, or any school team, or in the Debate club.
3. I founded a tutoring club for the school, but we don't do shit.
4. I have a comparatively moderate IQ, which sucks, because people with high IQs can easily hack competitive exams.

...I will apply for Princeton, and if I don't get into Princeton, either, then I would apply for Harvard, or Stanford.

I want to go to the best college, graduate, take an internship in CERN, get a PhD, write several scientific papers, get critical acclaim, and win the Nobel Prize.

Meanwhile that'll happen, I want to get signed to Hopeless, Rise, or Fueled By Ramen, record 4 albums, go for a worldwide tour, become rich.

And while that'll happen, I want to write bestsellers (I'm already working on one. It's called 'The Tears of a Clown', and it's about an aspiring scientist who fails miserably at the pursuit to happiness, and becomes severely depressed), date a really beautiful girl, who's actually smart, and also interesting, marry her, have as many kids as she wants.

See, I've got it all figured out.

The hard thing, however, is making all of this happen.

I memorized the derivation for Kinetic energy and Potential energy, and the Law of Conservation of Energy. Then, I studied some thermodynamics.

After I was done studying, I kept my books away, and I started writing my book, from where I last left off.

I wrote three pages, then I hit the writers' block, again, and I shut off my MacBook Pro.

I had pizza for dinner, and I went to bed, shortly after that. I tried to sleep, but I couldn't.

Insomnia, another side effect of depression.

I closed my eyes, shut them tight, and I eliminated any source of light in my room.

At 11:30, my phone rang. I wasn't asleep, so I wasn't pissed.

"Hi."

That voice, it screws me up.

A: "Hey."
R: "Sally told me you were depressed."
A: "How does Sally know that?"
R: "Everyone does."

I laughed, nervously.

A: "*beep*"
R: "Do you want to talk about it?"
A: "No, Robin."
R: "Tell me. I'm here for you. Why are you depressed?"

I wish I knew, Robin. I wish.

I closed my eyes, and let my heart do the talking.

A: "I just feel empty."
R: "What is it that'll make you feel, well, non-empty? Do you know?"
A: "Not really. I just mess everything up. And that makes me feel even emptier. And all this sorrow piles up. And it starts burning, inside. It practically hurts. I'm glad you're there for me. I see all these perfect people, and it reminds me how hard I try to be perfect. But it doesn't ever work… I should stop rambling, now."

Robin didn't reply. I waited for 5 minutes, in utter silence.

A: "So, how are you, Robin?"

Silence.

A: "How do you feel?"

More silence.

A: "Please say something, Robin."

I felt emptier. This silence was driving me crazier.

A: "I love you, Robin."

She said nothing. I could hear her breathing, but she said nothing. She didn't know what to say to that. Obviously, she didn't feel the same way. It's okay, I guess. No, who am I kidding? It's not. It hurts.

Time to end this.

A: "*beep* it. I'm just done. Have a good life, Robin. Bye."

I hung up on her, and I covered my head with my pillow. I wanted to cry. It felt like I was crying. My eyes were hot. No tears came out, though. So, I wasn't crying. I just felt this overwhelming desolation come cover me.

It really hurt. And not metaphorically. It actually hurt. Somewhere inside me, I felt pain. And it wasn't the kind of pain you get when you're sick, or when you wonder why the baseball bat is getting bigger, until it hits you. It felt like heartbreak. I just never thought it literally hurts. I felt like a hurricane deafened me. It just tore me apart.

Robin called me again.

R: "Holy crap. I'm sorry. You... Oh, god. I'm so sorry. And stupid. AAH. I'm sorry for not saying anything, Adam. Please."

I wanted to cry so badly. I didn't want to stay awake. I didn't want to sleep.

A: "I should go. Please forget me. Bye, forever."

I heard Robin sigh, and then she sobbed. She tried to hide it, but I heard her cry.

R: "Fresh start?"
A: "No, I'm sorry."
R: "I don't believe in forever."
A: "I do."

She sobbed, again. I felt even worse, now that I made her cry.

R: "Why are you sorry, when there's no reason to be?"
A: "There are a million reasons. I'm sorry for loving you."

She let out another sob.

R: "Not to me."

A: "Yes, to you."

R: "Adam, don't feel sorry for anything, okay? I don't like it. It makes me feel guilty, and I'm guilty, anyway, about everything."

A: "Why are you guilty?"

R: "You don't know me, do you?"

A: "I manage to mess everything up. I messed us up, Robin."

R: "That's human nature. You talk as if you're the only person who's ever messed anything up. No one's perfect. It's okay."

I sighed.

A: "You are."

R: "You don't know me at all."

A: "I used to."

R: "I'm the opposite of perfection. Everyone has their own definition of perfection. And very conveniently, I don't fit to any of them."

A: "You fit mine."

She started crying again. I felt the worst I had, in a long time.

R: "People change. I did, too, you don't know if I'm the same."

A: "I really wish we were together. So, I could make you see yourself the way I wish you could. But you can't always get what you want."

R: "You don't know me."

A: "I wish I did. I really do, Robin."

R: "I make a terrible person to be with, you'd rather be alone."

Yeah, alone. That's working out so well.

A: "You know, when you called, before, I felt so happy, inside. I felt happy, for the first time, in months. And it just hurts that you'll never feel the same way. I just adore you. And it's making me go insane."

I heard Robin sob, and then she laughed, lightly.

R: "I'm glad I made you happy, I thought you got mad. I'm sorry. I'll call more often if you want."

I rubbed my eyes.

A: "No, it's fine. It's better if we don't talk, again. I see it, now."

She started to say something, but then she paused. She didn't speak for a while.

R: "How do you know I don't or won't feel the same way? You can't just assume negative things, expecting them to be true, eventually, they do come true, and it's how this world works, according to me."
A: "You're too good for me."
R: "You're doing it again."

A: "I used to fantasize kissing you, Robin. I still do, sometimes. I actually loved you. Like, REALLY loved you. You don't know how it feels."

R: "Really?"

A: "Yeah."

R: "But why?"

A: "You are perfect to me. I already told you, so many times. I was rooting for you and I… So, tell me now. You hate me, don't you?"

R: "I don't."

A: "Liar."

R: "Imagine me looking you straight in your eyes. That type of look that creeps you out, and makes you want to look away. Yes, that look. Imagine me looking at you, and saying I'm not lying."

A: "You don't ever make me want to look away. I love you. Just, please don't fake it."

R: "Fake what?"

I didn't know what I meant by it. I just meant something. I was going mad. My eyes hurt.

A: "It."

R: "I won't."

A: "Thank you."

R: "Welcome."

I smiled. I think she smiles, too.

R: "I have to go to sleep now. I need to wake up early."

A: "If this isn't love, how do I get out?"
R: "What?"

I smiled, and chuckled.

A: "Nothing. Goodnight. Sweet dreams."

I don't know what Robin Chuckles was made of.

I wish I knew who made her.

Because no matter what, she always managed to make me feel like shit.

I can't let this kill me.

HANTAYHO

It was nine in the morning, when I heard a knock on the door. I wish it was death, just staring at my face, but alas, it wasn't.

My parents were gone for somebody's wedding, and I was glad they didn't take me.

I washed my face, and ran, to open the door, as somebody knocked, again.

And God damn it, I wish I could disappear. I wish I didn't exist. Because that, that hurt like hell.

"Hello, Adam."

As these two words haunted every little node inside me, I faintly replied,

"Hello, Robin."

I wanted to go to the Grand Canyon, scream my lungs out; cry, even.

A: "What're you doing here?"
R: "Talking to you."
A: "I'm sorry, okay? I can't keep doing this. I can't let this kill me."
R: "I don't care, Adam. You need to g-"

A: "-I hope you understand. I'm so broken. I feel so wretched. And I can't keep feeling like this."
R: "I still have the card you made me in 5th Grade."
A: "I still have yours. We could have been great, Robin. I still love you. But whatever. Yeah."

She held my arm, and kissed my cheek. I looked at her, and into her eyes.

She giggled.

R: "Just eat some blueberry yogurt. It'll all be alright."
A: "No, it won't. And you'll never get it."
R: "I get it, Adam."
A: "You can't save me."
R: "…"
A: "I'm gone forever."

I just walked off. I didn't even close the door.

I went to my room, and I started crying.

Finally. Crying.

It tore me apart, but it felt great.

Screw you, Adam.
Yeah, screw you, Adam.

I heard the door close, and I wished Robin came inside. I wish she came into my room, and kissed me, and I wish I could hold her, and keep kissing her. I wish I could hold her hand, and I wish that we went for a walk, and we kept kissing.

I heard the door close, and Robin left. That's what really happened.

Drink bleach.

~~~~~~

No, I still couldn't bring myself to do it.

I dialed 1-800-273-TALK.

"Hi."
"Greetings. You have reached The Scientific, Lembor-Kelph."
"Uh, pardon."
"Greetings. You have reached T.S.L.K."
"Um, won't you ask what my name is?"
"You are Adam Viper Somervell Timberlake. Aged 14. You must be calling for the internship program."

Modern technology never seems to surprise me. How do they know my full name? (My dad just wanted me to have a lengthy name, so he added some crappy middle names to my birth certificate, and I really, really hate it. I never tell my full name to anyone.)

"I want to kill myself."
"You want to skill yourself? I know, you do. That's what the internship is for."

It didn't seem like a suicide hotline at all.

I looked at my phone's screen. Oh, crap. I dialed 1-800-273-TSLK by mistake.

"Adam, I have signed you up for the internship program. You have to show up everyday, early morning, okay?"
"Um… wait… what is the internship for?"
"Key breakthroughs, and practicality of theoretical physics."
"Whoa. Really?"
"Yeah, really."
"…Uh…"
"Tomorrow, at 6. Bye."

…And he hung up on me.

What the heck did just happen?

HANGOVER 1

"Wake up! Wake up! Wake up!"

* GROAN *

"Wake up! Young man, you have a seminar to go to!"

Oh, right. I overslept again. 5:40 a.m. Shit.

Oh, right. I had accidentally signed up for The Scientific, Lumber-Something internship. Tomorrow, at 6, the man had told me.

I took a shower, and I don't have time to spare, for the details. My dad kept instructing me, about how to behave at the seminar. I tightened my laces, and my dad and I ran towards the car. My dad looked so excited. I wish I could make him this proud more often.

The car accelerated, just like my hopes, about making it, and surviving; and I reached, just in time. 5:56 a.m.

My dad knew the directions, so I figured that they must have got through to him, and they would have told him the address.

We drove through a boulevard, and my dad was a great driver, so I wasn't afraid of us jarring into thorny bushes.

There was just a metropolitan, in the middle of nowhere. Right in the center of the metropolitan, there was a huge building.

I entered the huge building, while I mouthed "bye" to my dad, and he waved at me. The building was huge. The building was gigantic.

Wow. This must be as tall as the Burj Khalifa.
Shut up. It's not that tall.

It looked like the Lumber-Something Company owned the whole building, because on the top of the building, it said T.S.L.K., in big, bold, gold letters. I went inside, and walked through the vast, automatic door. A security guard searched my body for bombs, and I went through a metal detector, and they used some Magnetic Field security techniques, until a guide led me to the center room.

A man in an unflinching, grey suit approached the podium, in the center.
"Dear Future-Interns,
My name is Dr. Stephen Kelph. A lot of you might ask... 'Is it Stephen with a "ph"?' Well, no. It's Stephen, with a PhD..."

He waited until the audience stopped laughing.

"...You are all here, because you signed up for our Internship program. This, I assure you, is going to be an extra-ordinary experience. I, personally, am fond of aspiring scientists, like some of you. If you've come here, just for fun, well, that's fine. Just take this seriously. We aspire, and aspire for, and to the best.

As to share what we will be doing, these upcoming days; we will be indulging in various undertakings.

The rest will be explained, later.
Thank you all for coming, and have a great day."

I didn't notice the overwhelming number of people in the audience, before.

So many people are here.
Of course. That's the way everything is.
Yeah. So much competition.
You sound exactly like your father. And don't get me wrong; it's a good thing.
Yeah. I need to matter.
Yeah.
I need to make myself matter.
Yeah.
I need to be remembered. I need to matter.

I heard a guy (with a ludicrous goatee, and glasses) say to his friend,

"Dude, there are so many people signing up for this shit!"

His friend, a girl (wearing a really long T-shirt, and glasses) replied,

"No, most of the people around us already work here. I asked some dude who works here, and he told me that about 100 people have signed up for this intern-shit."

"Ugh. Dude, wanna split?"

"Yeah, duh?"

I saw a man in a lab coat staring at me. He had shaved half of his face, and the other half was relatively hairy. He approached me, and said,

"Greetings, Adam. Good seeing you here."

I immediately recognized his voice. It was the man from yesterday, the one who signed me up for this.

"Hi."

"Are you ready to skill yourself?"

"Oh, yeah."

"Cool."

"Cool."

He gave me 'I'll-look-out-for-you' look, and I gave him a 'thank-you-so-much' look, which looked like a monkey making faces at an infant zoo-visitor.

I looked around, and saw hundreds of people, just swarming around, like bees, ready to sting. Most of them wore lab coats, or badges, or both, so it was easy to distinguish between new interns, and employees.

I saw so many hipsters, who just came here to click selfies. I also saw many of them leave, and it made me happy.

I grabbed a donut, from the center table, and I chomped on it.
Umm… sweet strawberry goodness.

I saw a lighted sign, that said 'EXIT', and I followed it.

I wish life had an EXIT sign.
I saw someone who looked very familiar. Sally. It was Sally. I tried to run past her, before she could see me, but she did see me, and screamed,
    "Hi, Adam!"

Shit. Crap.

    A: "Hi, Sally."
    S: "What're you doing here?"
    A: "I was just attending a seminar for an internship program-"
    S: "-Cool! I'm here shopping, with my bestie."
    A: "That's cool. There are shops here?"
    S: "Yeah, right over there."
    Sally pointed towards another building, right next to the T.S.L.K. tower.
    A: "Oh, nice."
    S: "Yeah, hehehe."
    A: "Yeah, so…"
    S: "I gotta look for Selena."
    A: "You're here with Selena?"

S: "Oh, yeah. You want to meet her, don't you? Of course you do."

A: "No!"

Before I could dissent against it, Sally held my hand, and dragged me through a dozen folks, and called out for Selena. Once she did fid Selena, she whispered something in her ear, and Selena waved at me, and said,

"Hey, Adam!"

I'm pretty sure I sounded like a rat,

A: "Hi."

S: "You look cute."

I knew that Sally had made Selena do this, and that the both of them would be particularly enjoying this. I would have just turned back, and ran away, but my dad got me an Etiquette book for my 10th birthday, and forced me to read it, so I made it a point to say,

A: "Thank you."

S: "You're welcome, cute stuff."

Selena was really pretty. Long, straight, blonde hair, with green-grey eyes. She was really pretty.

I glared at Sally, and she chuckled, and I said,

"Well, I'm gonna go, now."

Shortly after that, my dad came to pick me up.

He asked me how it was, and I said that it was fine.

How bad could this internship be?
VERY.
No, it might be beneficial.
Nice point.
You should go.
Okay.

"So, how was the seminar, young man?"
"It was nice."
"Hm. What did they tell you?"
"Motivational stuff."
"Hm. Okay. Good."
"Hm. Where to, next?"
"Let's grab breakfast, and then go home."
"Okey dokey."

We went to a restaurant called 'Sand-Witch', and we ordered a 'Big-Witch', and we divided it into two, and shared it. My dad inquired from the cashier about when they founded the restaurant, and he was all like,
"It's been a month, sir. Yeah."

My dad made me look at the bill, and he was excessively happy, because the total bill said '$4.50', when it actually had to be '$6.00'.

He quickly took out his credit card, and swiped it, before they revised the total bill. And he said, "Sand-Witch? More like Sand-my-Bitch!"

And we laughed for about three minutes.

We very swiftly ran towards the Blue Ford Fusion we called a car, and fastened our seatbelts. A man we recognized from the restaurant came, and knocked on the window. And we were petrified. My dad gave me a shit-he's-gonna-take-$1.50-from-us-now look, and I gave him an oh-my-god-you-are-right kind of look, but all the guy did was return my dad's credit card.

My dad made me swear not to tell my mom about our little detour to the restaurant, as she would have gotten mad, as she had already prepared breakfast for us, so when we reached back home, I said that I had a big stomachache and couldn't eat anything. My dad said that he had a stomachache, too.

▬ ▬

HANUARYEH

I didn't go to school, today.

I didn't feel like going. I didn't want to face any more fake 'friends' who bitched about me, behind my back. The concept of having friends who just pretended to be my friends scares me. That makes me feel so glad that I have people like Digboi and Sidnee, who genuinely care about me. But that scared me even more. The thought of them pitying me. Being my friends, only because they didn't want me to kill myself. The whole notion gave me shivers.

My dad woke me up at 5, and I didn't even complain. I remembered that I wasn't going to go to school, anyway, and that would stain my perfect attendance, which was not a big achievement, anyway, but I still liked the idea of having 100% in something. My dad told me that it's okay to miss school, once in a while, if it's for a noble cause, like going to an internship program.

I showered, and after I dried myself off, I wore my clothes, and my dad gave me a ride to the T.S.L.K. tower.

ACDC was playing on the radio.

I'm on my highway to hell.

I attended the first day of the internship program at the T.S.L.K. tower. They gave us a few lectures on how we could practically do anything, with just a few great ideas, and supplies that they'd provide us with. I liked the place, actually. It was pretty brilliant. The thing I liked the most about, was that Dr. Kelph, the co-founder and CEO of T.S.L.K., Incorporated, directly gave us those lectures, instead of asking someone else to do it. He seemed like a very kind, and benevolent man.

I formulated another theory, after I realized that my previous theory was nothing but crap. This one made much more sense. My theory, 'The Theory of Wormholes, Black holes, and How It Leads to Time Travel' worked on the ideas of super symmetry in our universe (I say our universe, because I firmly believe in the idea of multiple universes), or in any given universe, had Black holes, and those Black holes did, in fact, have an ending. The endings are nothing but portals, i.e. the complete opposite of Black holes, i.e. Wormholes. And these portals, or Wormholes, were most probably the closest we've ever gotten to find the pathways for Time Travel.

None of the other interns did actually write scientific papers, as we weren't required to, and were busy putting corndogs in the microwaves, or hooking up in the anti-gravity room, because they think that doing it in zero gravity is 'out of the world'.

I was scribbling down my postulates, when Dr. Kelph appeared behind me, and said,
    "Hey there, Adam. What are you working on?"

The idea of Dr. Kelph memorizing the names of every intern amazed me. I liked Dr. Kelph quite a lot. I aspire to grow up to be a scientist like him.

    "I'm just working on my theory, sir."
    "Hm. What about?"
    "Um… it's all just stupid."
    "C'mon. Show me."
    "Please don't mind the handwriting."

I handed him the papyrus, and he looked at it, thoroughly reading everything I had written. He read it about 4 times, and then, finally, said,
"Comewithme,rightnow."

Dr. Kelph signaled all the interns in the way to move, and I wanted to scream out,
    "Move, bitch, get out the way."

But I didn't, and just followed him. He seemed very determined.

We passed by some rooms, and labs, and puzzled scientists and the hallway seemed longer than ever. I felt like Eminem, and in that moment, seeing the path he paved for me, Dr. Kelph was Dr. Dre.

He put his hand on a print-recognition-security-system, and a sensor read his pupil, and then finally, after authorization was complete, the door slid open.

He smiled at me, and as we walked in, he went on,
"H e r e ' s w h a t w e ' r e g o n n a d o .
W e ' r e g o n n a w o r k o u t s o m e e q u a t i o n s,
findtheamountoflighttheBlackholewechoosehasa
b s o r b e d, o r w h a t e v e r e l s e i t h a s o b s o r b e d,
andthenfigureoutwhereallthatmattergoes."
"Is that even possible?"
"Here at T.S.L.K. Inc., anything is possible."

I stared at him, blankly, and he had this vivid smile on his face. So, I smiled back, and got ready to work.

▩ ▩

We didn't stop working. I didn't care if it was. We drove ourselves, recklessly, and we worked our asses off. Dr. Kelph gathered every 3rd year intern (if someone had managed to keep up with all the pressure that comes after the first year, it was a BIG deal), and demanded them all to formulate the equations.

I didn't even go home, Dr. Kelph convinced my mom to let me stay at the lab.

So, long story short, we did come up with an equation. An equation so long, that it would probably boggle your mind, and make you wish that you never bought this book, or asked a friend for it.

And it worked.

And for the first time in my life, I didn't feel disappointing.

Dr. Kelph had a meeting with his business partners, and they decided to send a satellite to the nearest Black hole, associated with a star called V 4641.

Dr. Kelph came out, took off his lab coat, tossed it in the air, and screamed,
  "Who's gonna change the world?"
And I grinned, and said,
  "We are!"

Dr. Kelph took me, and all the accompanying scientists out for a treat, in the best and most expensive restaurant of the city, where a glass of water cost $10. The food, however, was truly delicious. Words can't explain how good it was. When everybody left, Dr. Kelph took me to a bar nearby.

  "Treats on me, Adam. Drink whatever you want."
  "I don't drink, sir."
  "Really?"
  "Yeah, it's harmful."
  "Smart kid."

He called out to the bartender, and when the bartender asked us what I wanted, I said,
  "I'll have some H_2O."
  "I'll have some H_2O, too,"
Dr. Kelph said, instantly.

We stared at each other, and laughed, and Dr. Kelph even started crying. The bartender was puzzled, and looked at us as if we were retards.

We possibly were retards. Retarded scientists. I was happy. I was optimistic. It felt nice.

Dr. Kelph chuckled, and then said,
    "No, I'll just have a beer."

We sat in the corner booth, and Dr. Kelph kept cracking funny science jokes.

    "Never trust an atom. Atoms make up ever thing."
And,
    "A neutron walks into a bar; he asks the bartender: 'How much for a beer?' The bartender looks at him and says: 'For you, there's no charge.'"
And,
    "Why did the chicken cross the Mobius strip? To get to the same side."
And,
    "When asked if he believes in one God, a mathematician answered: 'Yes, I'm up to isomorphism.'"
And,
    "What is a dilemma? A lemma that proves two results."
And,
    "A scientist is experimenting on a frog. He says to the frog, 'jump frog', and the frog jumps. So he writes in his note pad: frog jumps on

command. Then he takes a scalpel and cuts one of the frog's front legs off, and once again says to the frog, 'Jump frog', and the frog jumps. So he writes in his note pad: when left front leg is removed, frog jumps on command. He takes the scalpel and cuts the other front leg off, and says to the frog, 'Jump frog', and the frog still jumps, so he writes in his note pad: when right front leg is removed, frog jumps on command. He then takes the scalpel and cuts off one of the frog's hind legs, and says to the frog, 'Jump frog', and though a little wobbly, the frog jumps on command. So he writes in his note pad: when right rear leg is removed, frog jumps on command. He then takes his scalpel and cuts off the last leg of the frog, and says, 'Jump frog'. The frog doesn't jump. The scientist lowers his head closer to the frog and yells, 'Jump frog, jump'. But the frog doesn't jump. So the scientist writes in his note pad: when left rear leg is removed, frog cannot hear."

And,

"Rene Descartes is sitting in a bar, having a drink. The bartender asks him if he would like another. "I think not," he says, and vanishes in a puff of logic."

That's when I saw her standing there. She had green eyes, and long, light brown hair. Dr. Kelph looked at me looking at her, and said,

"Go, get her, slick."

He was drunk. But he was fun. He was fun, even when he wasn't drunk.

He gave me some pep talk, which I'm sure was insignificant; because Dr. Kelph's wicked ways were from the 80s.

I somehow managed to walk up to her, and said,
"Hi. My name is Adam. What's your name?"
"Charlotte."
"Hm. I like your name… I really, really like your name."

I really, really liked her name.

"Are you drunk, Adam?"
"No, Charlotte, I'm not drunk. I'm not fond of drinking."
"Well, me neither."
"That's very nice."
"Yeah, haha."
"You're really pretty."
"Thanks. You aren't too bad, yourself."
"Ah, you're just shitting me."
"No, you're cute."

Cute. Cute annoyed the hell out of me. Cute was a substitution for 'Hey, you aren't ugly, but you aren't excessively hot, either'.

Almost every girl I had talked to, in the school had called me cute.

"Thank you."
"You're welcome."
"I think I like you."

I had just broken my two rules of talking to attractive girls;
1. Shut up.
2. Don't tell her you like her.
3. Really, shut up."
4. Don't compliment her eyes.

"Charlotte, I really like your eyes."
"Thanks, Adam."
"Will you be mine?"
She leaned in, and whispered in my ear,
"We'll see about that, cutie."

ACHIEVEMENT

I got into MIT. I was signed with Fearless Records, because my song 'Can Pigs Fly?' went viral on YouTube. I dated Charlotte for three months, broke up, the got back together, and I proposed last month. She said yes. We're engaged now. We're getting married next week. My book was an international bestseller.

The satellite reached the Black hole, and we gave it instructions in accordance with my theories. Wormholes were discovered. Dr. Kelph quit T.S.L.K. Inc., and co-founded another company with me. I'm a billionaire. I'm rich as a bitch. I've got the best fiancée in the world. I have a particle accelerator in my closet.

I won the Nobel Prize for Physics last year. And this year, too. I've got my own NBA team. I'm running for President. Campaigns are going well. Little kids look up to me. Hippies don't exist anymore. No one uses the word YOLO or SWAG anymore. Words like SWAG and SELFIE have been revoked from the dictionary. I haven't been depressed in six years. I've got a private jet, a ship, and three Porsches.

I'm not empty, anymore.

Seems too good to be true, doesn't it?

It is.

None of that really happened.

Told you, I was messed up.

Screw you, Adam.
Yeah, screw you, Adam.

～～～～～～～～～～～～～～～～～～～～～～

I heard the door close, and I wished Robin came inside. I wish she came into my room, and kissed me, and I wish I could hold her, and keep kissing her. I wish I could hold her hand, and I wish that we went for a walk, and we kept kissing.

I heard the door close, and Robin left. That's what really happened.

Drink bleach.

～～～～～～～～～～～～～～～～～～～～～～

No, I still couldn't bring myself to do it.

I dialed 1-800-273-TALK.

"Hi."

"Our servers are currently busy. All of our volunteers are spending time with their families. Please try again, later."

"Shit. Crap."

I felt hollow. So hollow.

I'm a hollow man.

Why do I feel like this?
You know why. Chemical imbalance.
There's gotta be something more. There's gotta be.
Well, there ain't. Shut up, and stop talking to me.
You're the only one I can talk to.
You're crazy, you know that? Shut up. I don't like talking to you. Bye.
Bye…

I felt so hollow. I am a hollow man.

We're all just hollow men. Hollow, and empty. Some of us pursue happiness. Some of us learn to live without happiness. Some of us can't make peace with it. So, we start burning, inside. Drowning. And before we know it, we're in too deep. And we can't keep holding on to nothing.

So, suicide helplines were busy.

I just went through thirteen more minutes of misery.

Complete misery.

I put on my headphones, and shut my eyes.

Twenty One Pilots was soothing.

I felt like Edward Scissorhands. Incomplete. An incomplete creation. An incomplete creation who couldn't do anything right.

Why do I mess everything up?

I finished my History assignment, when I felt a little better.

I had just finished answering the last question, when Sidnee called me.

S: "Hi."
A: "Hi."
S: "So, what's up?"
A: "Just doing my History homework. You?"
S: "Nothing, really."
A: "Cool."

S: "Adam, are you okay? You sound upset."
A: "Yeah…"
S: "Don't lie to me."

Sidnee always saw through my lies. Well, she did, mostly.

A: "I'm just figuring some crap out."
S: "What kind of crap?"
A: "I'm figuring out everything."
S: "Uh, huh. What have you figured out, yet?"
A: "I don't love Robin. I figured that out."
S: "Okay. Well I'm glad you're figuring stuff out for you, you know and all that crap. On a side not: You thought you loved Robin, earlier?"
A: "More than anything."
S: "Uh, huh. Okay."

I cleared my throat, and thought hard about what I was going to say next. I didn't want it to come out wrong.

A: "You shouldn't be so nice to me."
S: "What?"
A: "You shouldn't be nice to me, anymore."
S: "Why?"
A: "I… uh… don't deserve it."
S: "I like being nice to you. I'm like, genuinely nice to you."
A: "I know. You shouldn't."
S: "What? Why are you so depressed?"
A: "I'm not depressed. I'm just empty."
S: "Why?"

A: "I'm just a screw-up."

S: "Stop. Stop, okay? Your life isn't even bad."

I know. It's not. It's not bad. So many people have it worse. I don't know why, but I hate it, though.

S: "You've got this amazing life, okay."

A: "I…"

S: "You can't tell me that you have no friends. You do, okay? You have so many people who love you."

A: "I know. I just keep messing everything up."

S: "Huh. Like what? Your grades? 'B's aren't very bad. You say you're lonely. You aren't. Everybody's here for you."

A: "I know. My parents are disappointed in me…"

S: "I'm pretty sure they aren't."

A: "I'm disappointed in myself."

S: "You don't make any sense."

A: "I'm numb."

S: "Well, I have to go. Get your shit together. Bye."

A: "Bye."

JANUARY 12

I took a shower, and I wore my favorite yellow sweatshirt. This compound sentence was completely erratic, as:

1. My favorite sweatshirt was some other sweatshirt.
2. I had only one yellow sweatshirt.

But, it was somehow rational, as it really was my favorite yellow sweatshirt.

I used to wear it five times in a month, until I was waiting up for Sidnee, while she was talking to a senior who called me 'Awkward Yellow Banana Man', which I agree, is a completely bad-ass superhero name, but an insult, at the same time.

I tried making a movie called 'The Chronicles of Awkward Yellow Banana Man: The World is a Dangerous Place', back in Freshman Year, but it required too much money, and more than one actor, so that plan was unsuccessful.

I made a comic, called 'The Origins of The Awkward Yellow Banana Man', which sold no more than 3 copies.
I guess nobody fancies fruit-filled action encounters.

I wore a sweater, because it was very cold, today.

Not as cold as me, though.

As I walked in the class, I saw Digboi annoying Sidnee out of her skull. Ever since he watched those crappy Annoying Orange videos, he's lost his mind. Thea was talking to Allen.

I've known Allen since the 4th Grade. His parents are both architects, and his aunt used to work at CERN. That fact always astounded me. Allen was depressed, too, and he told me that he sees a psychiatrist, and that she helps him a lot. Allen was tall, and very, very skinny. He has good fighting skills, even though he plays badminton. He doesn't ever do his homework, but he gets decent grades. Allen used to cut, with a real knife, but he quit. No matter how much I ask, he doesn't tell me why he used to cut. The only person, who I think knows, is Thea, who Allen absolutely adores, but he often disguises it, by stating: 'I just like her'. I've told Allen about ten times to go ask her out, but he always says,

"No, man. I'm good being single."

Sometimes I really wanted Allen to be my best friend, and I wanted to be his. I have this feeling a lot, with a lot of people. I don't ever like being the second choice. I don't like being the substitute. My 'friends' only contact me when they have no one else to talk to. That saddens me.

Sometimes I really wanted Allen to be my best friend, and I wanted to be his. Maybe it was because he understood a part of me. A part of my sadness. He'd been going through that, too. He had his reasons, unlike me, who didn't even have any. He seemed lonely as well. Maybe we could talk it all out, and get better. He was already getting help, and he really was less sad. I'm so proud of him for stopping to harm himself.
I guess I never really tried hard enough for us to become closer.

He was one of the few people who got me.
Like, really got me.

I should have tried harder.

It's too late now, I guess.

I really liked Thea's hair. Thea was so beautiful. She wore spectacles, and so did Allen, but both of their spectacles were completely different. Just like them. They're both so different different.

Allen, or someone else, told me that Thea used to cut. I was really glad that she quit cutting.

I really want to know her better.
I really do.

I often feel jealous of Allen, because he's mostly hanging around Thea, and talking to her. She tells him all her deepest secrets, and that makes me wish that I were Allen.

Everyone knew that Allen really liked Thea, but Thea is often oblivious to that fact.

Oblivious.
I really like that word.

If you asked anyone, I was a hyperactive knucklehead. Because I'm always cracking the lamest jokes, sharing the most irrelevant facts, laughing in the wildest ways.

I hide my sorrow pretty well.

I'm always hiding behind the tears of a clown.

Once upon a time, I was not hollow.

I was more optimistic then ever.

I was not empty. No misery. No melancholy.

Once upon a time, I was enchanted.

I remember that day. I was holding her hands, and we were eating ice cream. Orange bar. I didn't like orange much, and neither did she, but we had it, anyway, because the vendor said that's the only one you could get for 50 cents.

I remember playing tag with her, and her dog, Taz, who frankly scared the shit out of me, but I played, anyway.

I remember her asking me to ride her bicycle, but I refused, because I didn't know how to ride a bicycle, and I didn't want her to see me fall.

I didn't want her to see me fall.

Little ten-year-old me first met little ten-year-old Robin in Grade 4.

I was a fat kid. I wore a sweater, and I ran around, anywhere I wanted to go. I had spectacles, too.
Robin was very shy, back then. She had shoulder length hair, and she didn't speak much. She was really pretty, but back then, before hitting puberty, everyone was.

I always wondered how she'd be like, but I didn't go strike up a conversation with her, and neither did she. Back then, boys hung out with boys, and girls hung out with girls. Any boy who was friends with girls was looked down upon. Times change, huh.

I admired her, when she recited a poem, in front of the class.

I admired her, when she looked out of the window, thought something, and smiled.

I admired her, when she got onto the bus, and waved goodbye to her mom.

I admired her, every time I looked at her.

I just wanted to know her better.

My best friend then, was eleven-year-old David. Back then he was pretty cool. He wasn't always trying to act cool. He wasn't always hitting on girls. He was innocent. Well, kind of.

I was a hardcore Ben 10 fan. The idea of having a device on your wrist that changed you into an alien intimidated me.
Every day, in recess, I would talk to other people who liked Ben-10. I would tell them my fantasies about being a hero, and they would, too. It was fun. I really liked them.

About that time, David started befriended the 'cool guys'. And shortly, he became one of them.

The 'cool guys' name my friends and I 'the Shit group', and we sincerely detested it, every time they called us that.

David lived right next to my house, so we spent a lot of time together, even after school. We played soccer, with a couple of other guys we befriended back in the 3rd Grade. Or, I went to David's place, and we watched Dragon-Ball Z movies, or we played Beyblade. He always had the coolest toys.

I had moved into the city when I was eight. My dad had got a new job, so we had to relocate.

The first time I met David was at the playground, near my new house. He had a bandage on his head. I didn't talk to him, that day. I just sat on the swing, and then went back home.

The next day, my first day of school, I met him at the bus stop. I didn't talk to him, that day; I just sat in the bus.

When I entered the class, and after Ms. Shelby introduced me to the class, I looked around, and saw David. Like I said, I didn't talk to him, that day.

My first day at school wasn't bad. I didn't cry, like most of the new kids cried. I didn't miss my parents, much.

I felt like I fit in. Back then, I did.

I didn't feel like an outcast.

———————————————————————

After two days, I finally did talk to David, and we became friends.

Little eleven-year-old David was a nice friend.

———————————————————————

After David was one of the 'cool guys', he changed. Gradually, he changed even more.

He started being bossy. He started being controlling.

Soon, he was dominant. He was an authoritarian.

He started cutting me off. Our friendship started dying.

After school, at the playground, if anyone didn't agree with him, David beat him up.

Back then, even a punch, or a push hurt. It didn't hurt much, physically, but it was humiliating, to get beat up by David, in front of everyone.

I started hating David.

I hate him, to this day.

I didn't know how, but by the time we went to the 5th grade, Robin and I were good friends.

I wonder if it was me, who walked up to her, and said,
"Hi, Robin, do you want to be my friend?"
Or if it were she, who walked up to me, and said,
"Hi, Adam, do you want to be my friend?"

Or was it something completely different. Something mutual.

But however it started, w started getting closer, week-by-week.

We talked all the time, in school, and when I came back home, she would call me, and we'd talk for at least fifty minutes.

Back then, little eleven-year-old me was happy.

Happy, and not torn.

Happy, and he wasn't contemplating suicide so often.

Happy, and he was falling in love with a girl, he thought was the one.

I spent all my time, during recess, talking to Robin. We would talk about the most stupid things. I would go on about last night's Ben 10 episode, and how amazing it was. She would go on about how much she loved dogs.

She had a beagle called Taz, and she cuddled with him a lot. I remember being extremely jealous. But then, I couldn't quite figure out what that feeling was.

I loved talking to her.

I thought I knew her.

I thought I knew her, like the back of my hand.

I thought she was the only one.

I started liking her, quite a lot. I blamed it on my damn hormones, but I couldn't quite shake off the feeling.

Then, we started drifting away.

Poles apart.

We were done. Hands down. Face down.
She became popular.

I was an outcast.

Fast forward to the 7th Grade. We talked very little. 'Hi's and 'Hello's.

By then, I was sure that I liked her.

I watched her walk away.
Right past me.

I was so invisible.

I watched her grow. I watched her smile. I watched
her laugh. I watched her gossip. I watched her,
from afar.

We still talked, but not as much as we used to.

We still had conversations, but those conversations
didn't last for more than ten minutes.

Little talks.
Little hearts, and little talks.

After a few months, I knew it.
I felt it.
At least, I thought I felt it.

I fell in love with her.

And, I fell hard.

All my friends told me to go, and ask her out.

Of course, I didn't do that, because I was a
castaway, and she was seamless.

That's when I got my heart broken for the first time.

Seventh grade.

That's also when I really started liking science.
I watched all of Stephen Hawking's lectures, well, all the ones I could find on YouTube.

Then, I got pissed at the seventh grade syllabus, and I started doing eighth grade science and math.

I felt smarter, after every Stephen Hawking and Richard Feynman book I read.

At first, I didn't understand half of what was written in them, but then, after I read two or three of them, and Wikipedia'd every term that I didn't understand, I started understanding all of it.

That's also about the time I decided to be a physicist, when I grew up.

Little did I know, that I would completely suck at math, and chemistry (even though I find chemistry really easy).

A year after that, I started making up rules.

Rules, for a better future.
   1. No dating.
   2. No drinking.

3. No drugs.
4. No porn.
5. No parties.
6. No spending money, unnecessarily.
7. No-doing-things-that'll-come-back-to-haunt-me.

I wish I didn't start to love Robin.
It still haunts me.

That's also about the time Robin started getting closer to a-tall-dude-who-played-the-guitar-and-had-really-nice-hair. They started dating, shortly.

I heard that Robin had her first kiss with him.

I hated on the guy for months. I did. How could someone be so cool, and have the best girl in the world as his girlfriend, at the same time?

Anyway, I couldn't bear the thought of her kissing him, so I put all my might into getting over her.

That was hard. Harder than a rock. Not harder than a diamond, but harder than a rock.

So, I'll cut the crap. I couldn't get over her.

But here's what I actually did do, to try and move on:
1. Read 'John Green' novels.
2. Read 'Ned Vizzini' novels.
3. Read 'Stephen Hawking' books.

4. Read 'Stephen King' novels.
5. Watched all the 'Scary Movies', and laughed a lot.
6. Read 'Twilight', but threw up after reading one chapter, so I stopped reading it.
7. Formed a band, with the lamest guys ever. (Not Digboi. I hadn't met Digboi, till then.)
8. Watched WWE, got too freaked out, stopped watching it.
9. Watched all Adam Sandler movies.
10. Started writing a book about this guy who was a superhuman, and had superpowers.
11. Wrote like three chapters, and discarded it.
12. Peed all over the urinal, when no one was looking.
13. Cut some of my hair, but nothing looked different, so said, 'Eh.'
14. Let Robin cut some of my hair, on the last day of school. (But that comes later.)

▬ ▬

Love is in the air.
Yeah, right.

I thought about it for a long time. Emphasis on 'long'. I thought for two weeks or so.

Then, I came to a decision.

Roses. *I'll give her roses.*

One of the lame guys in my band helped me out, quite a lot. He got me a bouquet of roses, because he knew how much I loved Robin, and that too, for free.

I would have gotten it myself, but then, my mom would've known, and she'd never have let it go. She'd tease me about it, for the rest of my life.

So, the lame guy, who I really shouldn't call lame, because he's one of my closest friends, so I'll call him by his real name, Ken Klux, called Robin for me.

Honestly, the moment he left to tell her to meet me, I freaked out.

I freaked out in such a way that everybody knew I was freaking out, or just that I went berserk.

I was shouting out 'Habeeboo', and I kept shouting, until everybody started glaring at me, and I calmed down, for a little while.

A war was going on, inside my head. I never felt so afraid. Well, I had. I always felt so afraid when I was at the doctors', and I was going to get vaccinated. My mom and dad had to hold me down, every time, for the doctor to inject the vaccine inside my bloodstream.

A little after five minutes of me going completely insane, Ken grinned at me, and I know what lay ahead.

He'd told Robin to come and meet me. I think she already knew what was going to happen, but I didn't care, much.

My heart stopped, when she walked through the door. Well, not literally. Damn these cheesy expressions.

She walked closer, and I could feel a rush of excitement, and fear just gush into me.

And then…

"Hi, Adam."

She smiled. I broke down, inside.
A: "…"
R: "…"
A: "Uh…"
R: "…"
A: "Um…"
R: "…"
A: "Happy… Valentine's Day."
R: "…"
A: "…"
R: "Uh, thanks."
A: "…"
R: "Same to you, too, Adam."

I choked.
I choked on the possibilities of Robin and I buried alive.

It seems pretty lame now. But when I was twelve, it hurt a lot. Young love, huh.

I tried to scream out, 'HELP', but I couldn't because I was choking. I was choking on something I'd eaten.

Ken saw me, and he panicked.

"CALL NINE-ONE-ONE!"
He shouted for help, but no one came, so Ken gave me a CPR.

He pumped my chest three times, and put his mouth on mine, and started blowing.
I wasn't sure if that was the solution to choking, but I let him do it, because choking didn't feel good.

No, I'm just kidding.
I choked, but not literally.

I choked.

I handed her the bouquet, and as I lost my self-confidence, I lost my dignity, as well.

Later, I heard that she gave the same roses I gave her to the-tall-dude-who-played-the-guitar-and-had-really-nice-hair.

What hurt the most was that I had spent so much time, planning with Ken Klux (who, I should clear this- was not affiliated with the KKK, he just had Klux for a surname), at his house.

We spent so much time talking about what we could do. We wanted to make it really special, so the love of our lives wouldn't forget. No, Ken didn't like Robin. This isn't Twilight. If you wanted to read about cheesy vampire crap with glitter and apples, you wouldn't have read this crap till here. Ken was in love with Andrea Stevens, who, unfortunately, was taller than Ken.

Andrea was pretty, and I wanted to know her better. I exchanged a few emails with her, but I didn't really talk to her in person. She was one of the first readers of the superhuman chronicles, so I liked her as a person.

Well, then again, I liked almost everybody, back then.

Ken had a broken-heart, too, because he gave a box of Ferrero Rocher to Andrea, and she said, "oh, thanks", and then gave the box to David Short. Ken had more of a broken-heart, because he didn't choke, unlike me, and told her how he felt. I can only imagine how a 'oh, thanks' felt, but later, I could feel it. Later.

After Valentine's Day, I started following my rules more seriously.

Not for long, though.

ROBIN DOESN'T DO HOLIDAY

It was a miracle, but somehow, Robin invited me to her thirteenth. Now, I got very excited. I got into my 'habeeboo' phase again.

After I had screamed my throat out, I started wondering what I was going to wear.

Suit and tie?
No.
Iron man tee?
No.
Batman sweatshirt?
No.
Banana outfit?
That'd be really cool, but no.

This went on, for a while.

I ended up wearing one of my dad's shirts, my black jeans, and my Chuck Taylors.

David's mom told my mom all about my crush on Robin, and David's and Ken's crush on Andrea, over the phone. My mom teased me a bit, but

then, she got two goldfish, and asked me to give
them to Robin for her birthday.

I thought about it, and it seemed like a good
birthday present.

I wrapped the fish bowl, and made Robin a card.

She smiled, as I looked around the club, to find
her. She had one of those smiles, which almost
made you melt. Almost.

She hugged me, as I handed her my present, very
carefully.

I wish we could stay like that.

But she pulled away, after nine seconds, and yes, I
was counting.

I could count, forever.

But it didn't last forever, so that's that.

I glanced around, and I saw him.

Him.

No, not the 'Him', in Power Puff Girls.

Him. Him, as in…
The-tall-dude-who-played-the-guitar-and-had-
really-nice-hair.

They'd broken up, weeks ago.

And seeing him there broke my heart, all over again.

R: "Adam, what'd you get me?"
A: "Fish."
R: "No, seriously. What'd you get me?"
A: "Fish."
R: "What?"

I met up with Samuel, who was the only one I knew well enough to strike up a conversation with. We fist-bumped, then high-fived, and then fist-bumped, again.

We were talking about some Xbox game he wanted me to buy, and I told him that I probably wouldn't buy it, because the only games I did have were Kinect Adventures, and the Gears of War trilogy, when Robin held my arm.

R: "You seriously got me fish."
A: "Yeah."
R: "Seriously."
A: "Umhum."

R: "That's so cool!"
A: "I'm glad you liked it."
R: "You're so cool!"

I couldn't help but smile. I must have been blushing, quite a lot, because my cheeks hurt.

She was smiling, too.

We kept looking at each other, and I looked into her eyes.

I really couldn't let her go.

A: "I love you."
R: "…"
A: "…"
R: "I… uh… love you too?"

And that put a bolt, right through my heart. My insides, torn up.

She didn't mean it. And she never would. Never.

ANOTHER VIEW MONTH

Ken and I wrote a comic book.

The adventures of Potato-Man.

It was about a boy, who was born with 47 chromosomes. (Humans are born with 46 chromosomes. Potatoes have 48 chromosomes. 47 chromosomes meant that the boy was a human-potato hybrid.)

It was supposed to be serious, but turned out to be funny.

Potato-Man had a catchphrase, like every other superhero.
I will take your dignity.

We wrote just three issues, and they were hysterical.

Hysterically sad how lame we were.

Somebody told me that Robin was going to another school, and after I confirmed the fact, I thought I would freak out. But, I didn't. And I was glad.

The rest of the year went by, relatively faster.

I got decent grades. Not good enough, just decent.

I felt myself wrecking up my future. A-Minuses weren't good enough.

I really wanted to get into MIT. I really wanted to be a scientist. I really wanted to earn at least $90,000 per year.

I thought about some things I could invent. I came up with designs of flying-cars, and oxygen-dispensers.

Soon, the source of my enchantment was lost.

▬ ▬

ROBIN'S LAST DAY

I wouldn't have even talked to her. I just made a farewell card, the day before, and asked Ken to give it to her.

I wouldn't have said farewell.

While everybody was outside, in the corridors, saying goodbye to Robin, I was inside class, reading The Grand Design.

And then she came.
The most enchanting thing.

A: "Robin, what're you doing?"
R: "I'm cutting your hair."
A: "Why?"
R: "Because it's my last day."
A: "Uh, huh."
R: "Haha."

A: "I love you."
R: "I love you, too."
A: "I'm gonna miss you so much, Robin."
R: "You will."
A: "You are the most enchanting thing."

She stopped cutting my hair.

I looked at her.

She looked at me.

I looked at her lips.

She looked at my lips.

I looked into her eyes.

She looked into my eyes.

I came closer.

She came closer.

I closed my eyes.

She hugged me.

I held her tight.

I wanted to kiss her, right then. But, I didn't. Because it wouldn't have mattered. I wouldn't have mattered.

She pulled away, and I said,
"Farewell, love."

She was the most enchanting thing.

HANGOVER

I woke up, dead.

At least, I wished I did.

I woke up alive.

But barely.

Because, I felt dead.

~~~~~~

~~I think I drank too much, last night.~~

I wish that were the case. But I follow my rules. I don't go to parties. And I'm not fond of killing my brain cells.

So, no, I did not have a hangover.

Though, I wish I did in fact, had hung over.

Hung over a rope.

But, that'd be too painful. Maybe. Maybe not. I wouldn't really know. I did not have enough pluck to try that.

~~~~~~

Sometimes, I think my music is all that I have, to keep me holding on.

These songs saved my life.

―――――――――――――――――――――

A few days ago, when I fell asleep, and I had a very dark dream.

Very dark.

A man is walking on a road. The streetlights aren't working, but only at this particular minute. Co-incidence? No. Fate? Yes. A man is walking on a road. He looks left. He looks right. He walks down the road. An empty road. So lonely. Out of a sudden, he hears a swift noise. Before he knows it, a car, running at the speed of 200 miles per hour, hits him. He gets hit, very badly. His arm breaks. His arm breaks off. He doesn't have a left arm, anymore. He's bleeding, badly. He just lost his left hand. The driver of the car must have paid homage to his guilty conscience, and gets out of his car. He asks the man he just hit, "Are you okay?" The man replies, faintly, "Yes. Can you give me a hand?"

This scared the hell out of me.

Damn it, Ken. Ken keeps sending subliminal thoughts to my head. He says he's the Illuminati, but I just roll my eyes.

I woke up alive.

But barely.

Because, I felt dead.

I got off my bed, and I drank the glass of milk my mom must have kept at my bedside, earlier. If only it was bleach.

I didn't want to go to school, but I knew I had to, anyway.

I went to the bathroom. I had a shower. I sang along to Just One Yesterday by Fall Out Boy. I got dressed. I wore my dad's blue Columbia sweatshirt, black jeans, and my grey sneakers. I put It's Kind ofa Funny Story in my bag, because I had told Digboi how good it was, and he wanted to read it. I wrote *MAN OVERBOARD* on my hand. I mouthed the word 'goodbye' to my mom, and waved to my dad. I punched myself in the face, so that I could feel pain, if nothing else.

The bus ride to school seemed so hasty, and debauched, that I wouldn't even bother you with the details. I just got off the bus, walked through the school gates, and faded into the pointless daily grind.

As I looked around, I couldn't help but wonder why.

What's the point of education, if we're all going to die?

What's the point of education, if I'm just going to kill myself?

~~~~~~

Sidnee caught up to me, and said,
"Hi."
I turned back, and sighed,
"Hello, there."
We walked together, to class. On the way, we met Thea.

Thea looked comely.

Her hair looked excessively curly, and I liked them so much.

I wanted to pull her closer, and wrap strands of her hair around my fingers.

But, of course, I did not, in fact, do that.

Never let your fear decide your fate.

I admired Thea, ever since last year. She really was intimidating.

She was so daunting.

She was somewhat unpredictable. Somewhat unstoppable.

I was jaded.

I was burned.

I was burned, and burnt.

I was burned, and burnt, and burned out.

I was burned, and burnt, and burned out, and blurry.

I was burned, and burnt, and burned out, and blurry, and blurred out.

I looked at Thea, and I realized I had been staring at her. She blankly stared back at me, smiled, and turned back towards Sidnee, to answer her question.

If only we were alone. I would possess your heart,
Thea.

I was just sitting, doing my Economics work, when
the person behind me passed me a chit. I asked:
"Who's it from?"
He stared at me, and mumbled:
"I dunno. Shuddup."

Hey, Adam. I'm back, again. Miss me?
-Anonymous

I had almost forgotten about 'my anonymous'.
She/he/it hadn't written to me in a while. Wait. Is
she/he/it in the class?

I looked around.

I'm done with this crap.

If she/he/it doesn't want me to know, fine, then.

I crumpled the small piece of disgraceful paper,
and threw it in the bin, in front of me.

Bull's eye.

I sighed, as the bell rang, and the period ended.

Everybody is a hypocrite.

We study about poverty.

We talk about changing the world.

We know about what's wrong with the world.

We are asked to empathize with the poor. The unfortunate.

They ask us to be thankful for what we have.

What DO I have?

The answer is clear.
Nothing to live for.

No one is perfect, until you fall in love with her.

I can vouch for that.

Really?
Really.

I feel so scarred.

I feel so scared.

Scared of everything I've seen, or known, all my life.

Scared of the unknown

I'm scared of myself.

Scared of these suicidal thoughts.

Scared of the thought of knowing what'd happen to the people who think they love me, if I kill myself.

I wish I could wipe out the fear.

But this fear's part of the only things that's left with me.

Dignity, long gone.

My life is made up of 'I'm sorry'. I feel like I have to apologize to people, to things, to life itself. It's like, 'I'm sorry to be here'. I don't want to disturb anyone.

As I walked out of the class, I saw Thea. She was talking to Allen, again. All I could make out of their conversation, was *genocide* and *massacre*.

I'm not being melodramatic. Allen actually used those words.

I really, really coveted to go talk to Thea, but I knew that I'd vacillate, and she'd prefer to talk to Allen, anyway.

So, I just walked past them.

I passed by Digboi, and high-fived him.

Ken caught up to me, and said,
    "Hey, ma homie."

He hugged me, and I patted him back.

    A: "Hi."
    K: "What up?"
    A: "Nothing. Just going to French class."
    K: "Did you hear about the guy whose entire left side was cut off? He's all right now!"
    A: "Oh, okay."
    K: "Dude, are you fine? It was supposed to be hilarious!"

It wasn't that funny. I just smiled.

    A: "Yeah, I'm fine."
    K: "You sure?"
    A: "Yeah."
    K: "Oh, oh, man, I got the best Batman comic book, ever."

A: "Oh, nice."
K: "I'll show it to you."
A: "Okay."

I followed him, and he took the comic out of his locker.

And yeah, it really was the best Batman comic book, ever.

It blew my mind.

I hadn't talked to Ken in a really long time. I wanted to make up for the lost time, and I told him so.

He said that I should go over to his place. I agreed.

We hugged, and then he skipped away.

Sidnee and I had French together, so I waited for her to show up, and then I went inside.

S: "So, what's up?"
A: "Nothing…"
S: "Tell me!"

I looked down, and breathed out, quickly:
    "I might like Thea."

Sidnee looked at me, in surprise.

S: "What?"
A: "Nothing."
S: "Adam, tell me."
A: "It's nothing."
S: "Adam, tell me. Please, tell me? Tell me. Adam, tell me!"
A: "I might like Thea."
S: "Uh huh."
A: "Hm."
S: "Can I tell her?"
A: "No!"
S: "Please? You know, we're besties, and I tell her everything!"
A: "I know. Just please don't tell her."
S: "Okay."
A: "Okay."

We were taught about 'Si Clauses', and the 'Imparfait' and 'Conditionnel Present' tenses.

I like French. It's an interesting language. It's fun, too. Besides, it'll really help me to know how to speak French, if I actually go ahead, and work at CERN.

I thought that Sidnee would freak out when I told her that I liked Thea, and she did. She didn't freak out much, though, and I was pleased.

S: "So, Adam, tell me!"

A: "Tell you what, Sidnee?"

S: "When did you start liking Thea?"

A: "Ever since the Christmas carnival, last year."

S: "The one with the horrible bands?"

A: "Yeah. The one with the horrible bands."

S: "Wait! I thought you liked Robin, back then."

A: "Well, I thought I did. Turns out, I didn't."

S: "Uh huh."

A: "Hm."

S: "Cool."

A: "Cool."

S: "…"

A: "…"

S: "Well, can I please tell Thea?"

A: "No."

S: "Please?"

A: "NO."

S: "Okay."

I walked out of the conversation, partly because I couldn't be part of that conversation, anymore, and partly because I was laughing at myself for liking such an amazing girl, and not knowing it, all this while.

As I walked away, Sidnee yelled towards my direction,

"Go talk to Thea!"

I smiled, and I kept walking away.

Every time I wonder why I admire Thea, I wait till it's night, and I look up at the stars. Then, I know.

She shines, bright, like a red giant.

Red giant, as in a species of stars, not literally 'red giant'.

She is so venerable.

Often, when Allen and Thea or Sidnee and Thea are having a conversation, I listen to them, from behind.

Now that the thought of actually going ahead and talking to her comes to my mind, it worries me.

I can't do it.

A couple of periods passed, like a million strangers passing by a homeless man, with a look of disgust and pity. Not that both of these things can be compared.

All the small things that tear us apart.
It scares me.

Ken came hopping, and I mean it, hopping towards me, during lunch.

I wasn't surprised, though.

A: "Hey, Ken."

K: "Hey, man. What's up?"

A: "Nothing."

K: "Oh, cool."

A: "What about you?"

K: "I'm just chillin' with my man Adam."

A: "Ken, you do know that I'm the one you're talking to, right?"

K: "Yeah, man."

A: "Okay."

K: "Dude, Andrea's dating someone."

A: "What? Who?"

K: "I don't know, yet."

A: "Oh."

K: "Yeah."

A: "I'm so sorry, man."

K: "It's… fine, man."

A: "I told you. You should've asked her out."

K: "Yeah… it doesn't matter now."

A: "Well, I hope they break up soon."

K: "Me too."

K: "So, dude, you wanna hear a joke?"

A: "Um, sure."

K: "What do you say to a cripple while going to a movie?"

A: "What?"

K: "Leg's go!"

I laugh, quite a lot.

K: "I have more."
A: "Go on."
K: "What do you say to a cripple, before he goes on the stage, to share a speech?"
A: "Something to do with legs?"
K: "Break a leg!"

I laugh a lot.

K: "I have more."
A: "Keep going, Ken."
K: "What is a cripple's favorite toy company?"
A: "LEGO?"
K: "Yeah! You got it!"

Ken and I 'thug-hugged', which is hugging normally, while cupping your hands while hugging, and thumping on the person-you're-hugging 's back.

Ken skipped away, while humming 'Let's Get Ridiculous' by RedFoo.

I smiled.

Ken's really cool.
Yeah. He deserves better friends than you.
I know.
Good.
I don't deserve any friends at all.
Stop wallowing in self pity. It's not about deserving people. The thing is, you don't need

friends. Just study, go to college, and be successful. That's all that matters.

I'm sorry.

Good. You should be.

Man, I keep telling Sidnee to stop being friends with me.

Why?

Because I don't deserve her.

Good move.

But she never really listens to me.

Well, then she's stupid.

She's anything but stupid.

Well, then she's just unwise.

A bit.

I wanted to find Thea, and try to talk to her, but it didn't actually occur, yet.

I ate a donut, and then I walked the corridors, in hope of finding Thea, or Digboi, or Sidnee, or even Ken, for that matter, to talk to.

I found no one, and somewhat startlingly, I was delighted, because if I didn't talk to anyone, I wouldn't mess anything up.

It was getting really, really cold.

I could feel my nose freeze. I should have worn gloves, but I didn't, see I just thanked fiction, and rubbed my hands together.

Then I put on my hood, and put my hands in my pocket.

I liked winters, and I liked them better than summers, but I still liked late springs better.

Here's why I don't like summers, much:
1. Girls who've just hit puberty wear without-sleeves, and their grizzly bear hair is visible. Plain gross. I know. Shallow. But that's how I really feel about it.
2. Everyone smells, as everyone sweats a lot.
3. Physical contact with anyone feels uncivilized.
4. Playing basketball is difficult, as the sunlight blocks the view of the ball.
5. Couples lick the same ice creams, and that upsets me, a bit.
6. Fat kids' man-breasts are VERY clearly visible. It's not even funny.
7. Nipple-squeezes hurt a lot.
8. I feel like taking off my shirt sometimes, when it gets really hot, but then I remember how weird it is to actually see people do it (Henderson does it, very often). Hence, I don't do it.
9. Ken has nothing better to do, so he rubs off his sweat on me, which, yes, is very, very horrid.

10. If I have too much chocolate, cocoa, or coffee, my nose starts bleeding, a lot. (It happens in winters, too, but more so, in summers.)
11. I don't get to cover my awful haircuts, by wearing beanies.
12. No matter how much deodorant I put on, the fragrance fades away.
13. It reminds me of Robin, somehow. Maybe it's because of the color the leaves of the trees turn. That's her favorite.

I don't know why, but I always feel worthless. All the time. It's not a temporary thing. It goes on, and on, forever, and ever.

A chronic illness comes in the form of despair.

I wish I had a chronic illness.

A severe chronic illness.

Something like Cancer.

Something that wouldn't go away. Like my worthlessness.

Not something treatable.

Something permanent.

Something that'd give me a reason to hate my life.

Something that'd explain why I feel like shit, all the time.

Something that'd kill me.

━━━━━━━━━━━━━━━━━━━━━━━━━━━━━━━━

I didn't find Digboi.
I didn't find Sidnee.
I didn't find Ken.
I found Thea, but I let her pass me by, because she was with one of her other friends.

I gave up looking, and I took out a piece of paper from my pocket, and wrote another postulate of my theory on Infinite Parallel and Opposite Universes.

Allen looked at what I was writing, and then said,
    Al: "Hi. What're you doing?"
    A: "Nothing, just writing a postulate."
    Al: "Oh, cool. What about?"

I explained to all to him.

    Al: "Hm… this is interesting.
    A: "Thanks."
    Al: "You're very welcome."
    A: "I need to ask you something."
    Al: "What is it?"

A: "Allen, how much do you love Thea?"

Al: "…"

A: "I'll tell you who I like, if you tell me."

Al: "A lot."

I smiled, and then, suddenly, Allen said,

Al: "Now, tell me who you like."

A: "Thea."

Al: "Really?"

A: "Yeah."

Allen gave me a blank smile, and then started laughing.

After a while, I said,

"She's perfect."

Allen grinned at me. That grin was the Allen grin. He always grinned like this whenever he heard or talked about something that interested him.

"I know."

The bell rang, and both of us rushed to our classes.

I had Biology, next.

I looked forward to go to Biology, because Thea, Allen, Sidnee, and I, all took it.

I went inside the classroom, and sat on my usual seat (first row, first column, from the door), and that was where I sit in every class.

It must have been a miracle, because the teacher was absent, and she rarely ever was.

Allen took the seat behind Thea, and they were talking about something, again.

Sidnee sat behind me, and said,
"Did you talk to Thea?"

    A: "No."
    S: "Go. Talk to her."
    A: "I can't."
    S: "Why?"
    A: "It's hard."
    S: "Why?"
    A: "I'm afraid I'll come across as lame to her."
    S: "She thinks you're cool. Go talk to her."
    A: "Also, Allen already is talking to her."
    S: "Oh gosh."

Sidnee got up, and rushed off to Allen. She screamed at him,
    "Oh my god, Allen! You keep talking to Thea all the time! Go sit in the front. Let Adam talk to her."

Sidnee needn't have done that.

Sidnee, however, was the best best friend ever.

Sidnee came back, and smiled, and I smiled back. Then, she said,
    "Go. Talk to Thea."

I took the seat beside Thea, as Allen got up, and left.

She looked at me, and I tried to smile. She smiled, too. She looked really pretty. Her cheeks looked slightly red.
I thought of what to say to her, and she was waiting for me to say something.

I couldn't say anything.

I opened my notebook, tore out a page, and started writing down the name of every punk rock band I liked.

After I felt that it looked nice, I gave it to Thea.

    T: "Wow. This is really cool."
    A: "Thanks."
    T: "This looks really cool!"

I looked at it, once again.

    A: "You can have it."
    T: "Really?"
    A: "Yeah."
    T: "Oh, thank you."

After about five minutes of me staring at her, in silence, she said,
    "What's up?"

I shook my head, and stood quiet for a while. Then, I said, quickly,
"I'm seriously addicted to Rise Against."

Thea smiled, and looked at me, and then smiled again.

T: "Really? They aren't a bad thing to be addicted to. I think it's healthy."
I smiled, too.
A: "Savior is killing me. And in a good way."
T: "There is a good way to be killed?"
A: "That was a metaphor. However, yeah, there are good ways to die, such as laughing to death."
T: "Unfortunately that would mean something getting internally damaged which would mean that the pain would be excruciating. So I don't really think that's a good way to go."

I was falling in love with Thea. It was gonna last for some time, at least.

A: "Well. Thank you."
T: "Thank me? For what?"
A: "For being so cool."
T: "Hehe. Anytime. Oh, thanks for the band drawing thing you let me have. It's really cool."
I looked into her eyes.
A: "Always, Thea. You know, I love you."
T: "Heh. Always? A cheesy bastard, aren't ya? And I'm sure, as hell, love doesn't exist. But still, you know, I love you, too."

I wonder if she meant it. She probably didn't. Thea couldn't possibly say, 'I love you, too' and mean it. She probably meant in a 'friends' kind of way.

When I think there's nothing lamer to say, I go ahead and say the lamest thing possible.

A: "I'm no more cheesier than a double-cheese pizza. And I'm sure that it does. We just gotta find it. I love you. Like really, love you."
T: "You think you're going to find it? Answer me this. How do you find something that only happily exists in movies?"

I thought about it for a while. It was a very valid question. It was. I really was.

A: "It doesn't just exist in movies. It actually exists. There's more to dating, or having a crush, or having *beep*, or whatever. It's basically having a ton of Oxytocin in you, and a person you really like. That's love."
T: "There is more to everything. But to find a person you really like and to find a person you love is a bit different isn't it?"
I nodded.
A: "I wouldn't really know. I thought I loved this girl, but I might have been wrong."
T: "Well, uh, shit happens?"
Then, Thea and I snickered.
A: "Yeah, I guess so."

T: "Why were you wrong?"

A: "Unrequited feelings."

T: "Why didn't you tell her?"

A: "I did tell her. She just didn't care."

T: "Why do you mean she didn't care?"

A: "She said she loved me, too, but it was clear she didn't mean it, and she still makes me feel like shit. She makes me cry sometimes…"

T: "What did she do to make you cry? And most of all she probably doesn't deserve you. Why does she make you feel like shit?"

A: "No. I don't deserve her. And I've figured that out. I'm possibly still in love with her. She asks what's wrong with me, and I tell her everything, and she doesn't respond. Then, after I while, she calls me back, but I felt miserable. She came over the day after, but I made her leave. I'm done with her."

T: "Bullshit. I bet you deserve her more than you know. Do you know why she didn't respond then?"

A: "I really don't. I don't know. Maybe she found someone else to talk to. Well, I'm never going to talk to her, again."

Silence. I just admired Thea's beauty. I'm sure she must have been crept out by me staring at her.

A: "Then, there's this other girl I admire, but I feel so distant to her."

T: "Whoa, there's another one?"

A: "Yeah, haha."

T: "Why so distant? To her, I mean."

I looked down.

A: "I feel distant because the people she loves surround her, and all of them are perfect. And so is she. We don't even talk much. I just wish we did."

T: "How do you know she loves them?"

A: "She's just so intimidating. And pretty. And amazing. And lovable. Who wouldn't love her?"

T: "Why don't you guys talk much? You want to, then do it."

A:"Yeah, I try to talk to her, but she doesn't seem interested at all."

T: "Make her interested. What makes her so intimidating?"

A: "Everything. I love her hair. She's kind. She's really pretty. We like the same stuff…How do I make her interested?"

T: "You like the same stuff. Talk to her about that…

Get to know her find out what she REALLY likes.

And just give a shit about her I guess."

A: "I give so many shits about her, I might have diarrhea. She really likes MCR. And punk rock."

T: " P u n k   r o c k ,   e h ? RESPECT. MCR? DOUBLE RESPECT.   If that's a thing…"

I don't know how to explain how beautiful she was. She was beautiful, in that moment, as well as, all the time. The way she talked and smiled blew my mind. I could get used to this. It was nice. She was nice.

A: "So, yeah. How are you?"
T: "I'm just as good as it gets. How are you?"
A: "Yeah, okay is the best I can be."
T: "I think okay is the best we all can be."
A: "Yes."

The substitute teacher came in. I don't know what his name was, but he looked severely strict, and he yelled at Thea and I to shut up and take out our books.

We solved some questions that the strict substitution teacher with a grey moustache gave us.

I solved some, but they were easy as hell, so I didn't feel like doing them. Neither did Thea. She hummed a song. I wonder which one it was. Then, she smiled, and whispered:
    "Aren't bass lines the sexiest thing ever?"
    "THEY SO FREAKING ARE."
That came out louder than I wanted it too.

Silence, again.

Make her interested.

    "I play the bass on my rhythm guitar."

Just how lame can you be, man?

T: "You play guitar? That's amazing."
A: "Yeah, I do. Guess what my band's called."
T: "YOU HAVE A BAND? What's your band called?"
A: "Eternal Subside. Yep, it's Digboi and I."
T: "Not a bad name, too. Very emo. Impressive. Who's the lead singer?"
A: "Je suis."
T: "Cool."
A: "Hm."

The strict substitution teacher with a grey moustache started staring at us, and he was gonna scream soon enough, so we shut up for three minutes.

"But seriously, dude, go talk to her,"
she whispered.

A: "She's the Boss. Tell me what to do with her. I might potentially adore her."
T: "Just tell her, I guess."
A: "Okay… How?"
T: "Walk up to her, and tell her how you feel."

I felt a jolt, and I do not know what or who caused it, but I stood even closer to Thea, and…

A: "I love you."
T: "Yeah, like that."

I looked down, and then, at her.

A: "I love you, Thea."

T: "Why?"

A: "You're the one."

T: "Oh. Wait. It's me? I'm not any of those things you said, Adam."

A: "You're perfect."

T: "No. I'm not."

I couldn't stop looking at her.

A: "It's you. I'm sorry. I'm so sorry."

She didn't say anything. She looked away.

After a while, she put down the book she buried her face in.

She looked at me. I started thawing.

T: "Why are you sorry, Adam? You haven't done anything wrong. It's me. I should have said something. Anything. I am the one who should be sorry. So I am really sorry if I did anything to hurt you."

A: "No, I'm sorry. And you didn't hurt me, at all. Are we cool?"

T: "You have to tell me why you're sorry."

A: "I'm sorry for messing this up."

T: "Messing what up?"

A: "I just shouldn't have told you."

T: "It's okay you know. Nothing is messed up."

A: "Oh, okay. I'm so glad it isn't."

T: "Hey, me too."

I tried to smile, again, and I did smile, and it felt good. She smiled, slightly. I waited for a moment, and the bell rang.

Partly, I was glad the period was over.

I knew Thea hated me.

―――――――――――――――――――――

Even if she didn't hate me, yet, she probably thought I was annoying.

And she would have absolutely hated that conversation.

It wasn't hard to talk to Thea.

It was scary.

Scary, how I could mess things up, so much.

Sidnee and I shared a lot of classes, so, during Physics, she asked me,
"How was your talk with Thea?"

    A: "It was nice."
    S: "Oh, cool."
    A: "I might have messed it up, again."
    S: "What? I'm sure you didn't."
    A: "I think I did."

S: "Look, you did not. I know Thea. She likes talking to you."
A: "No, she doesn't."
S: "I'm her bestie, okay? I know she does."
A: "Hm. Okay. I like her so much."
S: "Uh huh."
A: "Yeah."
S: "Go talk to her, then."
A: "Now?"
S: "Not now. Later. After school. Okay?"
A: "Okay."

Then, the Physics teacher yelled at us, and told us to shut up, too. She was probably having an affair with the strict substitution teacher with a grey moustache.

I looked at the blackboard, and made myself understand the concept.

I took down some notes, and then closed my notebook.

I wanted to think of this brilliant idea.

Think of it, and then make it happen.

I want to change the world.

There are two thoughts that dominate my life.

First, the thought of changing the world.
Second, the thought of killing myself.

If the first one doesn't work out, there's always the
second one.

It's funny how one word can contradict it's
complete existence.

Always.

I went to Allen, just as the period ended, and
demanded him to tell me everything about Thea.

He didn't say anything, and just left.

I didn't mind that.

In fact, it'd be nice, if everyone who knew me did
that.

Just walk away.

Or perhaps, I should.

Walk away.

School ended, and Sidnee nudged me to talk to Thea, again.

I waited for Thea to come by, and when she did, I let her go.

I heard Allen ask her,
"Is Massacre over?"

I wanted to stop her right there, and ask what Massacre meant. But, I didn't do that, because I was scared.

Scared of messing it up, again.

I watched her go.
I felt my insides screaming at me.

I let her go.

I got on the bus, and sat next to Ronnie. I hoped he'd make me feel better.

He smiled, as I sat down next to him, and as if he knew how dismal I felt, he said,
"I like to eat my excretion."

I laughed, a bit. I wanted him to go on, and he did, making me feel a little less low.

"S-H-I-T, I eat shit for breakfast and lunch, but for dinner, I eat paint thinner."

Ronnie was my guardian angel. And I was so thankful. He went on,

"Ayo senorita, you should make me a pizza. Double cheese, and extra shit. Yummy, yummy."

This reminded me of a song I heard a while ago, probably influenced by Lil Wayne.

N*gg*s like pizza, yeah n*gg*s like pizza.
(x40)

Ham, Chicken, Beef, Pepperoni and double Cheese
Can somebody pass me the oregano, please?

After a moment of silence, Ronnie asked me, "Don't you like peeing?"

My conversations with Ronnie are so impulsive and heartfelt, I swear.

   A: "I do. I love peeing."
   R: "Me too. It feels so good!"
   A: "I know! It feels nice."
   R: "There's this girl in my class who likes me."
   A: "Oho, Ronnie. That's cool."
   R: "Yeah, I know."
   A: "Haha. You're so modest."
   R: "Do you have a girlfriend?"

A: "Nah."

R: "How come?"

A: "Because I'm… me."

R: "Oh, come on. You're the coolest person I know."

A: "Thanks, Ronnie. I'm sure you'll be dating a hottie, two years down the line."

R: "Yeah, I know."

A: "Haha."

R: "Well, does anyone like you?"

A: "I don't think so. I like someone, though."

R: "Huh. Who?"

A: "Just a girl I know."

R: "Is she cool?"

A: "Yeah, really cool. And pretty, too."

It wouldn't have mattered to me if Thea were less pretty. She would still have captured my hopeless, desperate heart, if she were as awesome as she is, now.

R: "How much do you like her?"

A: "A lot."

R: "Do you like talking to her?"

A: "I do. I really do. We don't talk much, though."

R: "Why?"

A: "Because I'm scared, Ronnie."

R: "Don't be scared. Just be yourself around her."

A: "Look at you, being a wingman and all."

R: "Haha, I'm a p*mp, yo."

I wanted to just hug Ronnie, but I wouldn't want him to ask me if I were coming on to him. So, I didn't hug him.

By this time, I had realized that I was a cuddler.

The hours at home passed by, like tides in a sea. Faint, lonely, a bit cold.

My mom had to meet with a client, so she made me a carrot-cabbage-mayonnaise sandwich, and left.

I thought about what to do.

After thinking for fifteen minutes, I decided to compose a song.

I lift up my guitar, turned up the bass on my amp. Then, while I played some tunes on the seventeenth and eighteenth frets, I thought of some wicked rhymes. But, the rhymes didn't go with the kind of music I was playing, so I changed the theme of the song, to what I cared about, most: Thea.

You make me feel like there's still hope.
Am I wrong? Am I wrong? Nope.

After I played that awful piece of music, I wanted to shoot myself in the eye.

―――――――――――――――――――――――――――――

There's nothing I can do right.

I always mess up everything.

―――――――――――――――――――――――――――――

I slapped myself in the face, and then turned on the TV, to watch Sherlock.

Holy freaking crap.

Mindcrap.

Sherlock is the best show, ever.

No words, at all.

―――――――――――――――――――――――――――――

After I watched all of the third season, I wanted more Sherlock.

But I couldn't watch more, because I realized it was 11, already.

I went to bed, and closed my head, trying to sleep.

The bad thing about insomnia is that you can't sleep.

The good thing about insomnia is that you have plenty of time to think about, well, everything.

I did think about everything that I adored.

Thea.

~~~~~~

I closed my eyes, and I wanted to sleep, for the first time in my life.

I had a dream.

After such a long while.

It's a rainy day.
Everybody is carrying an umbrella, but me.
I'm standing in the rain, all alone.
I'm soaking wet, but I like it.
I try to smile, as people pass me by, but I can't get myself to do it.
I see a thousand strangers.
I look around.
Loneliness.
Until, I see a familiar face.
She smiles at me.
Thea smiles at me.

I try to smile back at her, and I do, somehow.
She comes closer.
I want to get even closer, but I restrain myself from doing it.
She comes closer.
Even more closer.
"Show me your scars," I say.
"Okay," she replies.
She looks at me, and lifts her sleeve up.
Thirteen little scars.
A perfect, but shattered girl.
I lean in.
She grabs my waist.
I hold her face.
She comes as close as she can.
I look into her eyes.
We kiss.

JANUARY 18

The moment I woke up, I felt sad.

Sad, because my dream had ended.

Sad, because I knew it would never occur in reality. Why couldn't reality be something that could easily be bent?

I did what I do, everyday.

Drink milk, shower, brush, comb, bye, bus, laugh at Ronnie, reach school, hi, hi, hello, what's up, high-five, high-five, fist-bump, thug-hug, get beat up, like getting beat up, hate school, hate myself, contemplate suicide, follow Thea, see Sidnee leave Thea I alone, try to talk to Thea, fail miserably, cry deeply, hear Thea laugh, genuinely smile, wish you could hug Thea, slap myself in the face, make Thea laugh even more, like the fact that she's laughing, eat a donut, eat another donut, eat another donut, get high, do weird shit, jerk off with Ken (no, not m*st*rb*t**n. Jerk off, as in, doing weird crap to others), have a rap battle with Ken, laugh at how sucky it was, tell Digboi to write some riffs, hit Digboi in the stomach, get pep talks from Sidnee, give pep talks to Ken, talk to Allen about my theory, remind to myself that Allen is really, really cool, draw manga in Chemistry, write another song about Thea, show it to Digboi, hear Digboi laugh after reading it, hit Digboi, again, follow Thea, again, tap her shoulder, say hi, listen to her say hi, follow Sidnee's advice, crack 'that's what she said' jokes, listen to Thea laugh, melt inside, want to hug her, even tighter, resist the temptation, write another chapter of my book, draw blink-182's logo on my hand, show it to Sidnee, see Sidnee smile, feel good about it, find Ken, give him a pep talk, again, give Ken a thug hug, prevent Allen from dozing off, during Biology, talk about Hitler, during History, talk about worthless shit, myself.

I constantly keep thinking about the dream I had yesternight.

I saw Thea drawing something in her notebook. I went near her, and I looked at what she was making.

She was making eyes. They weren't as beautiful as hers, but they still were really pretty.

She noticed that I was standing beside her, and she smiled.

> K: "Yo, wanna hear a joke?"
> A: "Hm… okay."
> K: "What did the sea say to the ocean?"
> A: "…"
> K: "Nothing, they just waved."

A: "Oh, okay."
K: "You okay, Adam?"
A: "Never been better."
K: "NO. SHUT UP."
A: "…"
K: "I worry about you."

That's the last thing I want.

People to worry about me.

I hate myself even more, when people pity me.

I hate myself even more than when people pity me, when they worry, about me.

Worrying causes weariness.

I said to Ken,
    "Please don't worry. I'm fine."
    "You better be, ma man."

I smiled at him, and he gave me a hug.

Thank you so much, Ken.

Sidnee called Thea, and she stood up, looking around.

The way your hair swings over your eyes.

She spotted Sidnee, and waved at her, as she went towards her.

The motor in my head turns.

Ken snatches my notebook, and pushes me towards Thea.

Wanting you for such a long time.

I stumble, a bit, but I prevent myself from falling on Thea.

In my mind, a heart, a lesson to learn.

I smile, awkwardly, as I awkwardly stand near Thea.

Do do do do do do do do.
You'll never know,
I'm after you.

I plainly stare at her, thinking that I should probably say something, but I don't, because of my inadequate self-esteem.

Do do do do do do do do
You'll never know.

I kept looking at her, and even though I knew that she was probably freaked out, I kept doing it.

Her hair smelled very nice.

And you smell like,
How angels ought to smell.

After about five minutes of me looking at her, and
Thea waiting for me to say something to her, I
finally manage to say,
"I like your face. That's why I stare."

Thea just smiles, and begins to say thanks, but I cut
her off.
"I think I love you."

Thea says,

"No, you don't. You think you do, but you don't.
Nothing to love, in here. You don't even know
me."

A: "I'd love to know you."
T: "Well. I'd love to know you, too."
A: "Tell me everything about yourself, Thea."
T: "What's there to tell?"
A: "So much."
T: "Like what?"
A: "Do you still cut?"
T: "Wow. So direct."
A: "I'm sorry. I'm just... curious. You don't
have to tell me."
T: "No, it's okay."
A: "..."
T: "..."

A: "I'm sorry."

I didn't know what else to say.

I just stood there, like an idiot, after asking her if she still cut herself.

I hated myself even more.

She retorted,

"Have you seen my arms all month?"

A: "No…"
T: "…"
A: "I'm so sorry."
T: "It's alright. Don't worry."
A: "I shouldn't have asked you that."
T: "It's fine."
A: "I think of doing it, too, sometimes."
T: "Cutting?"
A: "Yeah."
T: "Why?"
A: "…"
T: "You don't need to answer."
A: "…"
T: "…'
A: "I mess everything up."
T: "So do I."
A: "No, you don't understand. You are perfect."
T: "No, I'm not."
A: "You are. You are the most perfect person I've ever met. Other than maybe, Kim."

T: "No, I'm not... WHOA. Kim from Scott Pilgrim Versus The *beep*ing World?"
A: "Yes."
T: "Holy shit. Respect!"

Thea was so adorable.

A: "I love you, Thea. So much."
T: "I'm sorry."
A: "For what?"
T: "I'm sorry for not telling you that I'm dating someone."

Is this the real life, or is it just fantasy?
"Oh."

⁘⁘⁘⁘⁘⁘⁘⁘⁘⁘⁘⁘⁘⁘⁘⁘⁘⁘⁘⁘⁘⁘⁘⁘⁘⁘⁘⁘⁘⁘⁘⁘⁘⁘⁘⁘⁘⁘⁘

I asked Sidnee whom Thea was dating, but she told me she didn't know.

I asked Allen whom Thea was dating, but he told me he didn't know.

I went around, killing time, trying to figure out who it could be.

I wondered if she got back together with any of her ex-boyfriends.

Aaron

Prefect.
Could run for President, in the future.
Number 09 on the soccer team.
Well built.
Thea asked him out.
He said no.
He asked Thea out, the day after that.
They dated for two weeks.
Thea broke up with him, in twenty seconds, during lunch break.
Potential not-so-ex-anymore.

Stephen

Aces all math tests.
Very high IQ.
Part of the school badminton team.
Liked Thea for a very long time, and asked her out.
Thea said no, because she liked Darth, at the time.
Made Thea feel like shit about rejecting him, she cried, and finally said yes to him.
They started dating.
Forgot to do anything for Valentine's Day (not that Thea wanted him to do something).
Called up Digboi at the last moment, and told him to get a cheesy vampire book (Thea hates cheesy vampire books).
Thea had the flu, and didn't go to school, on Valentine's Day.
Got pissed at Thea.

Went back home, after school.
Logged into Facebook.
Abused Thea, quite a lot.
Thea asked him to calm down.
Looked for excuses.
"Sorry, Thea. That was my cousin."
Of course, she didn't buy it.
Apologized to Thea, a lot.
Thea stopped responding.
Thea broke up with him, in school, the next day.
Potential mathlete, but not not-so-ex-anymore.

Darth

Socialite.
Bassist of the school band.
Has nice hair.
Pretty cool guy.
Thea liked him for some while.
I think they dated, after she broke up with
Stephen. I'm not so sure if they did, though.
She broke up with him, after seven days.
Potential not-so-ex-anymore.

***

Sidnee said to me,
"Adam, I didn't even know if she was dating
someone. And we're supposed to be besties."

A: "Well…"
S: "…"
A: "I will just hate on the mystery guy."
S: "Uh huh."
A: "Hm."
S: "Good luck with that."
A: "Thanks."

After thirteen minutes of just thinking about this, I walked up to Thea, and asked her,

A: "Who are you dating?"
T: "Why do you want to know?"
A: "I'm just curious."
T: "…"
A: "…"
T: "Wouldn't it hurt you, if I told you?"
A: "No."
T: "Bullshit."
A: "It doesn't matter."
T: "Fine. I'm dating Derek."
A: "Shit. Crap. I swore to myself that I'd hate on the guy. But I can't hate on Derek."

Derek

Was in our school till last year.
Transferred into the best school in town.
Pretty good with computers.
Really talented pianist.
Really funny.
Really nice.
Kind of good looking.

Decent soccer player.

Lived three blocks away from Thea.

Was one of my really good friends, back in eighth grade. We wrote the script for the first season of an animated show we wanted to create, 'The Dope Show', an epic series about a fourteen-year-old kid, Dope (voiced by Derek) who had really bad luck (his birth parents died in a truck collision, when he was three days old, then he went to live with his aunt, who died three days later, due to severe constipation, then he was sent to live with his other aunt, who died, because she ate uncooked mushrooms, so on so forth; then, he is sent to live with his distant-uncle-and-aunt's, who have a son, Charles, and the moment Dope arrives, a bomb explodes in the neighborhood, and Charles' parents die). Charles (voiced by me) and Dope are sent to their great aunt and uncle's, who have no idea how to raise teenagers, and rename Charles, to call him Pope, just because it rhymes with Dope. Charles gets a girlfriend, Siena (voiced by Robin). Later, as the story sets in, it's revealed that their distant great uncle was a headbanger, but lost all his hair, and turned grumpy. The show was hilarious, and we had high hopes, but it didn't go anywhere. I designed some figures for the characters, and they were okay, but we failed to ever buy animation softwares, and go ahead with actually making a show.

Potential best-boyfriend-ever.

T: "Why can't you hate on Derek?"
A: "Because he's amazing."

T: "Oh, okay."

Digboi was calling out for me, so I waved to Thea, and followed Digboi.

Thea swiftly touched my shoulder, as she tried to catch up to me, and faintly said,
     "Adam, please don't tell Sidnee about the cutting. I don't want her to worry."

A: "I promise."
T: "Thank you."
A: "Always."
T: "Cheesy bastard, aren't you?"
A: "As cheesy as an extra cheese taco."

~~~~~~

The rest of the day passed away, like corpses in a graveyard.

Forgotten, rotten, from the top to the bottom.

NA NA NA NA NA NA NA NA NA NA NA
DRUGS, GIVE ME DRUGS, GIVE ME DRUGS
I DON'T NEED IT BUT I'LL SELL, WHAT YOU GOT?

AND WE CRAWL, AND WE CRAWL, AND WE CRAWL.

Ken, Henderson and I sang Na Na Na by My Chemical Romance, and Sidnee and Digboi frowned, upon us.

I went near Thea, and said,
  "Kiss me, you animal."
  "What?"
  "Nothing."
  "Okay."

EVERYBODY WANTS TO CHANGE THE
WORLD, BUT NO ONE WANTS TO DIE
WANT TO TRY, WANT TO TRY, WANT TO TRY,
WANT TO TRY?

THE UNNAMED

As I got off the bus, and walked towards my building, I thought about Thea, once again.

You break my heart, in a blink of an eye.

I hunched down, and tied my shoelaces. And that's when I saw him.

The dead of his eyes got to me.

The dead.

A: "Ken, come over to my place, as soon as you can."
K: "What the crap, man? I just got home."
A: "Please. Come here."
K: "Are you okay, man?"
A: "Please. I'm begging you. Come here."
K: "Adam, are you alright?"
A: "Yes. Just come here."
K: "Okay. Wait fo' fifteen minutes."
A: "Thank you."

I waited till he got here.

He asked me what was going on, and the moment I point it out to him, he stared blankly, in nowhere in particular, at first, and then back at me.

I didn't have to say anything.

After about six minutes or so, he broke the silence.

> K: "Are you sure he's not just sleeping?"
> A: "…Why would someone be sleeping in the yard?"
> K: "He could be a hobo."
> A: "He's wearing a freaking suit, man."
> K: "Well, maybe he's just passed out."
> A: "Quite a possibility."
> K: "Do you know him?"
> A: "No. I've never seen him before."
> K: "When, how'd you find him?"
> A: "I just got off the bus, and… wait. Is that poison?"
> K: "What? Where?"

I pointed towards the bottle, labeled Cyanide, and Ken gasped.

Silence, again.

A man was dead.

⸻

He had taken Cyanide, and killed himself.

In the yard.

Dead.

━━━━━━━━━━━━━━━━━━━━━━━━━━━

His eyes were closed, but I could see the dead, in them.

Maybe he couldn't hold on, anymore.

He finally broke.

No.

He didn't break.

He didn't even break even, or break out.

He just let go.

I want to let go.

━━━━━━━━━━━━━━━━━━━━━━━━━━━

By the science of deduction, I observed, and then inferred that he was in his twenties; somewhat well off, economically, but not emotionally; maybe someone was disappointed in him; he gave up, on everything; nothing seemed to get better.

It kills me when I remind myself how much I disappoint my parents.

Maybe something like that happened to him.

Maybe it killed him.

Killed.

For the first time in days, I felt horrible, again.

Horrible, and horrified.

~~~~~~

K: "Man, we should call the cops."
A: "I know, Ken."
K: "Call 911."
A: "You do it. I'm out of balance."
K: "Okay."

Ken dialled the three digits, and told them everything we knew about the man. Then, Ken and I got into the lift, quickly, and I knocked on my door.

Ken asked me if we should tell my mom about the suicide, but I said no, because it would freak her out.

If I went ahead, and told her, she would ask me if I were kidding, I'd say no, she'd ask me, again, I'd tell her to go down, and look for herself, she'd freak out, and call my dad, and I would end up getting a lecture about 'not committing suicide' or a 'he was stupid to do that' speech.

So, I just hugged my mom, and tried to wipe away my tears, before she saw them.

I showed Ken into my room, and we sat down on my bed.

We just stared at the floor, till he said,

> K: "So…"
> A: "So…"
> K: "Do you think he'll go to heaven? Or hell?"
> A: "Suicide. Hell. Then again, we live in Hell, and I don't believe in Heaven, or afterlife, for that matter."
> K: "…"
> A: "…"
> K: "I don't know what to say, man."
> A: "Me either, Ken."
> K: "So…"
> A: "…"
> K: "You want to talk about it?"
> A: "Are you screwing with me, right now?"
> K: "I'm just kidding."
> A: "Okay."

I looked at Ken, and Ken looked at me.

We felt a connection.

It felt like love.

I leaned in, and he leaned in, and we kissed.

…

No, not really.

That'd be a good plot twist, wouldn't it?

But no, I was in love with Thea, and Ken was in love with Andrea.

Besides, Ken and I would be platonic.

K: "Hey, Adam?"
A: "Yeah, Ken?"
K: "Does Andrea live nearby?"
A: "Yeah, matter of fact, she does. Three blocks from here."
K: "Oh my god. I wanna go and see her!"
A: "Hm. Okay. We can go."
K: "Really?"
A: "Really."

We were about to leave, when my mom made me stop, and asked Ken and I to eat the sandwiches she'd made for us.

So, we ate the sandwiches, somewhat delicious, and I hugged my mom, and Ken said thanks, and we left, for Ken's ultimate conquest: Andrea.

We took the path less traveled by, because Ken knew I couldn't handle seeing the dead guy, again.

I call him the dead guy.

How insensitive can I be?

Very.

One becomes insensitive, when he loses all hope.

No hope, here.

I wanted to say goodbye to the cruel world, but I couldn't do it, because I wasn't ready, yet.

Besides, I had to be the world's worst wingman, for now.

For Ken.
Death comes later.

So, we walked down the road, across the boulevard, and then, across the Cemetery.

A couple hours later, they would bring the dead guy here.

And he'll be as dead as everyone else.

That's all we can be, right?

Dead.

~~~~~~

Ken asked me, with a poker face,
"Do you believe in reincarnation?"

I replied, tranquilly,
"No. Once dead, always dead."

I don't believe in reincarnation, or life after death, but I do believe that when a dead person's atoms break down, they roam around, and finally form molecules and ions, and they make up another person.

Our brains are hardware and our minds are software. When our bodies fail our minds do the same thing a program does when a computer shuts down. It's gone. It no longer exists. Unless, if it's backed up, of course.

This makes no sense, but it does, too.

If consciousness ceases at death, how then are we experiencing the present at all?

If you do not exist prior to birth, and you also do not exist after death, how is it possible to be experiencing the present?

Since time is actually not linear, it is merely a perception, the fact that consciousness exists at any point in time at all suggests that it cannot be destroyed, otherwise we would have no memory of it, including in the present.

But, it appears as if we do, so, shut up, and help Ken possess Andrea's heart.
Okay, bye.
Bye.

I've never really been friends with Andrea.

We don't even do the occasional 'hi'-'hello'.

Ken told me he was a best friend to Andrea in the first grade, but then she became popular, in the seventh grade, and they got pulled apart.

I could relate with him too much.

But he hadn't given up, yet, and I was happy for him.

I'd be happier if Andrea felt the same way.

We stopped, when the light went red, then we ran through the zebra crossing, and I felt a twitch on my leg, and I fought it.

When I was ten, my parents took me to the physician. He acted all nice, and then, I realized that I was going to get vaccinated. So, I cried, and I begged my parents to let me not get a vaccination. But, apparently, it was very important for my immunity to get a DPT booster. So, they made me lie down, and pulled my jeans up, till my pelvis. I cried, harder, and my mom and dad held my arms, while the physician stuck a needle in my thigh. I screamed, and I could feel the aroma of my dad thinking that I was nothing but a sissy bastard, but then, I didn't know what bastard meant, and I just let the feeling pass. But it was harder to let the pain pass, so I cried all the way home. I cried, because while I was getting vaccinated, I felt something break inside me, and no, it wasn't me, yet, it felt like a needle. But every time I told my mom that, she said that I felt like that because I was not steady while getting vaccinated, and the needle got inclined. But it didn't break inside my leg. Now, often, when I run, I fell a twinge in my left leg, but I just shake that feeling off.

I wish I could do that with depression.

~~~~~~

"Where now, Genius?" asked Ken, while we were standing on an intersection point, which dissected into two roads.

A: "Um, left."
K: "Okay, man."

We walked for a half a mile, or so, and then I picked up some rocks.

K: "What're you doing, man?"
A: "Just picking up some rocks."
K: "Why?"
A: "Protection, if someone tries to kidnap us. Or if someone rapes us."
K: "Oh, okay."

He picked up some rocks, too, and we kept walking, till I recognized Andrea's house. The only reason why I knew it was hers is because I watched her get down here, everyday, from the bus.

A: "Here we are, Ken."
K: "Oh-my-god! OH-MY-GOD!"
A: "Why are we here, anyway?"
K: "Coz."
A: "Don't you 'coz' me.

Ken and I had this thing, where we would answer every question starting with 'why', by 'coz'.
For example:
  • Why are you so gay, Adam?
Coz.
  • Why are you so lame, Ken?
Coz.
  • Why are you humping this chair?
Coz.

A: "Tell me, Ken. Why are we here?"
K: "Andrea's leaving, man."
A: "What?"
K: "She's leaving town."
A: "Oh. I'm so sorry. When?"
K: "Tomorrow."
A: "Oh."
K: "What should I do, man? Shit. I can't do this. Let's go back."
A: "NO. We're way too close to walk away, now, Ken."
K: "What do you think I should do? Just knock on her door?"
A: "Yes."
K: "And what?"
A: "Say what I tell you."

I was hardly a romantic, but still more romantic than Ken. An ideal Valentine's Day gift, for him, was a lightsaber.

He thought for a while, and then asked me,
"Okay. What do I say?"

I cleared my throat, mostly for emphasis.

> A: "Hi, Andrea. I know you're leaving, and it
> kills me to say this, but I've loved you all these
> years, and I always will. I don't want these to be
> our last words, because I love you far too much
> for that. Please don't forget me."
> K: "Really?"
> A: "Yes."
> K: "Okay…"
> A: "GO."
> K: "Okay… no, I can't."

I slapped Ken on the face, and asked him to calm
down. I pushed him towards her porch, and he
stumbled. He regained his balance, and knocked
her door. I smiled at Ken, and hid behind the
bushes.

All I could hear, was Andrea saying,
"What are you doing here, Ken? … Well, come
in."

I waited for Ken to say what I told him to say,
maybe get a kiss from Andrea, and then come
back, smiling.

I waited for five minutes.

He did come out, and he looked weary.

A: "What happened Ken?"
K: "I messed up."
A: "What'd you say?"
K: "I said, 'Hi, Andrea, I know you're leaving tomorrow, and I just wanted to say goodbye.' And then, she said, 'Okay, bye.'"

I patted his back, and asked him to go back inside, and ask her for her number.
He was reluctant, at first, but then, he went inside, and got her number.

I asked him to copy down her number on his hand, and I took the piece of paper from him, and turned it over. Then, I took out a pen, and asked Ken to write down this:

So, dear, no matter how we part, I hold you sweetly in my head.
And if I do not miss a part of you, a part of me is dead.
If I can't love you as a lover, I will love you as a friend.
And I will lay a bed before you; keep you safe until the end.

He wrote it down, and asked me why I'd made him do it.

"Ken, start listening to my kinda music. You'll get it."

He shook his head, and handed me the note.

I went and pushed it through under Andrea's door.

I left the note, and walked back home, alongside Ken.

He said,
    "Thanks so much, man."

And I, I smiled, and said,

    "Always."

~~~~~~

When we reached back home, I made Ken listen to all of La Dispute's stuff, and of course, he liked 'Andria' the best.

Ken told me an idea for a short movie he was going to shoot, about assassins.

I gave him some ideas, like calling the bad assassin 'Bad-Ass.', and the good assassin 'Good-Ass.', but he rejected all my ideas, because he wanted the movie to be serious.

Then, Ken had to go, so I saw him off, till his driver came to pick him up.

~~~~~~

I was still jaded, after seeing the dead guy.

I felt jealous, somehow, somewhat.

Jealous?
Jealous.

I felt jealous, because he was dead. And I wanted to be dead.

Just end it all.

I wanted to talk to someone.

Someone who'd understand.

Sidnee couldn't understand. Neither could Digboi. Nor could Ken, for that matter.

Thea.

⸺⸺⸺⸺⸺⸺⸺⸺⸺⸺⸺⸺

I asked my mom if she could drop me off at Digboi's, to record a song. She told me to wait, because she had to make a call, but after five minutes, she said okay, and I grabbed the car keys.

My dad had been teaching me how to drive for the past few months, but my parents still weren't sure if I could handle driving, without getting any dents or scratches. Besides, we'd just bought the silver

Captiva, a month ago, from one of my dad's friends, who was moving to Singapore.

Thea lived nine miles away from Digboi, so after my mom dropped me off at Digboi's, I said, 'Hi' to Digboi, told him I'd just come to tell him to listen to La Dispute, he laughed, and then said okay, and then I said, 'Bye' to him.

I walked past a few of the mansions, owned by the stinking rich people. I wasn't poor, but I wasn't rich, either. My mom told me that we were upper-middle class. Whatever. It doesn't even matter. There's little nobility in poverty.

I saw a little kid, of about five years, playing with a little girl, who was probably his sister.

They looked really happy, and I thought about the last time I was that happy. Fourth grade, I think.

I pulled out my earphones, and I turned the volume, up high.

Hanging in the shadow of your halo
Oh no I sank to
So low
Time to go
Give me strength
So let me
Let me
Out of the
Bastard mirror

It makes me wary
Of my skin
And all that lies within
I'm envious
Of a snake because it
Can shed skins as it requires
Set me on fire
I will swim across the aquarium
To find where my broken body will lay.

I couldn't hear it, but I could feel the leaves, being crumpled, under my feet.

If only someone would crumple me like that.

Higher, higher
Take me higher
Purify me
Holy water put out my fire
Liar, liar
Our time is dire
Crucify me
Let death inspire me.

It was cold, and my hands were freezing, so I put them inside the holes of my pockets.

I wanted to fly away.

I wanted wings.

I wanted to fly away, on my wings, and keep flying, till I forgot how disappointing I was.

But, here I was, walking on a lonely road, towards the one I loved.

Correction.

The road wasn't lonely.

I just thought it was, until angry drivers honked at me, and abused me. I got off the road, and started walking on the side path, faint forest.

Hanging by the thread of your desire
Take it all
Take me home
Time is slow
Give me thought
And let it
Let it
Flow out the
Windowsill
Drown in the gin and pill
I'm victorious
Just like a lion as it roars
And in the jungle the roar echoes
Exasperated fire
I will lead an army and win all my wars
To make my broken body proud.

I almost stepped on a piece of shit.

Stupid dog owners and their stupid dogs.

Poop all over the place.

I skipped over the poop, and I landed on leaves.

Wet leaves are still better than poop.

Poop and pop (music), same thing.

I walked on a non-lonely road, and it was getting dark.

I saw some kids playing baseball in the park.

They looked happy, and seeing them happy, I smiled.

It was getting dark, and most kids were going home.

I wondered why my mom hadn't called me yet. The latest I'd ever stayed out of home was till eleven, on New Year's Eve.

My mom expects me to sleep at nine, everyday, but I go to bed at ten, at the earliest.

I felt sorry for my mom. She deserved the best son, ever, and she got the worst.

Sometimes, I wonder if my parents wonder how it's possible to have an off-spring so disappointing, in every way possible.

Last year, at an MUN, I was appointed Poland, and I won High-Commendation (mainly because all the other delegates were stupid, and basically incapable of handling a good debate with substantial points; and I had a resolution, with me being the only sponsor). That was the first award I'd ever won, except those worthless drawing and coloring competitions I'd won when I was seven.

So, my parents took me out to celebrate it.

It wasn't that big an achievement, anyway. It wasn't like I'd won Best Delegate or something.

So, as they bought coffee, cheering to my award, I felt even more disappointing, that this was the best I could do to make my parents proud.

The thing about depression is that it accelerates your feeling of being disappointing. It makes you feel like shit, over and over again.

I could be a happy kid, and as much as I wanted to be one, I couldn't, because I was worthless.

And worthless people don't deserve happiness.

They don't deserve sadness, either.

They deserve nothing.

Nothing at all.

I kept walking, and as it got darker, the headlights started shining.

A hundred cars must have passed me by. I would count, but I was lost in my music, so I didn't.

I saw a cut from the highway, so I took it.

I went towards the left, and this time, it was indeed, a lonely road.

A lonely road, in the dark.

There were streetlights, there, so I didn't quite trip and fall over roots of nearby trees.

I was close, and I knew it, as soon as I saw the sticker of the flower of life on the black mailbox.

Sempiternal.

I'm here.

I looked at her house.

Her pretty little house.

Her pretty little house, with a pretty little girl inside.

Her pretty little house, with a pretty little sad girl inside.

She is suicidal, and I know that, because I almost killed myself trying to talk to her, a few days ago.

Metaphorically speaking, of course.

It killed me to hang around, and wait for Thea to be alone.

I spent hours, just waiting, and looking at her beautiful face.

Her body, too, was perfect. I mean, I have nothing against plus sized girls, but Thea was in the swim team, so, she had a nice body.

After enough pep talks from Sidnee, and a joint initiative taken by all, who left Thea and I alone, every chance they got, I finally talked to her.

Initially, Sidnee dragged Thea and I out of the class for a walk.

Then, slowly, Sidnee slowed down, and then went back to class.

The first few minutes were awkwardly silent, but then, we started talking about Scott Pilgrim vs. The World, and how amazing Ramona was. Then, again, we came to the conclusion that Kim was the most amazing person of all time.

Then, we talked about how amazing Ken was, but how nobody knew it.

Then, I told her I loved her.

She smiled, and asked me why.

I told her why, and I told her that I'd already told her that so many times.

I don't remember what we talked about, after that, because what came after that will never leave my mind. It's like a memory so deeply burnt inside my soul. And that's coming from a non-spiritual, non-religious pessimist.

    A: "Thea, why do you cut?"
    T: "Why do you want to know?"
    A: "I'm sorry. You don't need to answer that."
    T: "It's fine. Why do you want to know?"
    A: "Because I care about you."
    T: "You hardly know me."

A: "Yeah. That's what everybody tells me. Everybody."

T: "I'm sorry, but-"

A: "-No, listen to me. I'm scared to let someone in, and I know how much it hurts when someone you love lets you down. I hate myself for doing that. Thea, I love you. Okay? I love every part of you. I frankly wouldn't care, even if you were a freaking pedophile."

T: "I want to die."

A: "So do I."

T: "I'm not just saying that."

A: "Yeah, me neither."

T: "I'm suicidal, Adam."

A: "I hope you don't kill yourself."

T: "Huh."

A: "If I could, I would kill myself, too."

T: "Why?"

A: "Because I hate myself."

T: "Why do you hate yourself?"

A: "I'm so disappointing. I mess everything up."

T: "Oh."

I looked at her.

A: "Do you want to sign a suicide pact?"

T: "Hell yeah."

A: "Okay?"

T: "Promise you won't ditch me?"

A: "Promise."

Then she hugged me, and I hugged her, tightly.

We kept walking, and then she started laughing.

She looked so pretty, when she laughed.

I smiled, and I waited for her to tell me why she was laughing.

> T: "You really wouldn't care if I was a pedophile?"
> A: "Nope."
> T: "Really?"
> A: "Well, maybe."

Then, we laughed. It felt so nice.

I wanted to lean in, and kiss her, but I didn't, because she had a boyfriend, and also, she would hate me for kissing her, because she probably thought I was disgusting.

I talked a lot to Allen, about Thea, too.

We talked about how perfect she was.

I asked him what 'massacre' and 'genocide' meant. Every time I heard Thea and Allen talk, I heard either one of these words.

He was disinclined to tell me, at first, but he told me, after I asked him again, and again, and maybe because he saw the look in my eyes.

Curiosity regarding something I adored.

He told me they were codenames.

'Massacre' meant 'cutting'.

'Genocide' meant 'suicidal thoughts'.

Allen laughed a bit, and told me that he told Thea to refer to Massacre as a guy, so if anyone heard them talking, they would think it's someone Thea liked. Then, he told me that Thea asked him to refer to Genocide as a girl, because it would be a very non-feminist thing if they didn't.

I looked at Allen, and I could tell how much in love he was, with her.

And I could tell he looked at me, and could tell how much in love I was, with her.

On New Year's Eve, I texted Thea, and she told me she broke up with Derek.

Then, my dad asked me to have dinner with the family, so I said goodbye.

The next day, Allen told me that Thea broke up with Derek, and I told him she already told me, and I asked him if he knew that she cuts, and Allen said that he didn't.

Maybe that's why they broke up. Maybe she couldn't let him in.

I just wish she'd let me in, someday.

I told Thea everything, in the following days.

I told her that my parents were probably disappointed in me, and it killed me to see the look in their eyes, which meant nothing other than sheer disappointed.
I told her that I wanted to push everyone away.

I told her that I knew she wanted to push everyone away, too, because she was tired of people worrying about her.

I asked her not to push me away.

I told her I loved her.

Now, I was here, at midnight, staring at a pretty house, with the love of my life inside.

I could have knocked on her door, and she'd probably come out, or let me in.

I could have called her, but I didn't have her number; I could have called Digboi and asked him for Thea's number.

But, I was here, at midnight, staring at a pretty house, with the love of my life inside.

I just looked at her house, from the outside.

Like a spirit, watching over the city.

I loved moments like these.

I loved moments when I didn't think anything.

Nothing at all.
My mind was empty, but I didn't feel empty, for a while.

And it'd been a while since I hadn't felt empty.

So, it was nice.

Nice, indeed.

I looked up, at the stars.

The sky was very clear.

Clear, like my mind.

I could spend hours, looking at the sky, knowing the fact that I was three yards away from eternal happiness.

Not that anything is eternal.

But, yes, I was three yards away from happiness for a long time.

I'd call Thea, tell her to come outside, tell her that I love her, again, and then hold her face and kiss her.

She'd hopefully kiss me back.

And after seven years, we'd get married.

And have kids.

As much as I wanted that to happen, I did not call her.

I knew she'd still be awake, because in Thea's case, it was just twelve o' clock.

Call her.
Uh, no. Don't wanna bother the love of my life.
Oh, shut up. Don't be a pussy and call her.
I can't. I don't want her to hate me.
Take a leap of faith.

Fine, gosh.

~~~~~~

"Hey."
"Hello, who's this?"
"Hi, it's Adam."
"Oh, hey. What's up?"
"Heh, um, funny story… I'm, um, right outside your house right now."

Thea called me in through her window.

A: "I'm sorry for being here so late. I'm s o r r y for being here at all."
T: "It's okay. Why are you here, though?"
A: "I just wanted to see you."
T: "Uh huh, okay."

Now I was regretting my decision, because she looked crept out.

She looked really pretty, even after midnight.

She had no make up on, and she wore a The Black Parade shirt, and light green shorts.

A: "Hey, Thea?"
T: "Yeah, what's up?"
A: "Let's talk all night."
T: "Cool."

I sat on the ground, and she lay awake in her bed, and I had the best night of my damn life.

T: "So, whatcha wanna talk about?"
A: "Tell me all about yourself."
T: "What do you wanna know?"
A: "Everything you want to tell me."
T: "Hm, ask me questions."
A: "Tell me about your sister?"

She sighed, and continued,

"My sister, huh? Okay, if you insist on knowing. Her name's Fianna, and she's in college. She got me hooked to punk rock, which is the only thing I'm thankful to her for. She gets by. I don't really know what else to say."

I smiled, and just stared at her. She was cute as hell. I could just stop, and watch her. All my life.

T: "I don't really know much about you."
A: (trying to mimic her) "What do you wanna know?"
T: "I dunno, just tell me more about yourself."
A: "Hm, let's see. I pretend to be pop punk, I'm just a kid who writes flimsy songs and books, I love science, and Taylor Swift, I get sad sometimes, and I'm desperately in love with you."
T: "Cool."
A: "Your turn."
T: "I'm Thea, I'm way more pop punk than you ever will   be, and I get sad sometimes, too."

I guess she was right, because she did have a lot of piercings, and mismatched socks and shoelaces, and torn jeans, and band tees.

A: "You look really pretty."
T: "Psh, no, you look prettier than me."

I blushed, even though I knew she was kidding. She was so sarcastic it was captivating.

We talked about school, and how we thought that Sidnee was lesbian because she never had a crush on any guy but Alex Gaskarth. We laughed a lot, and I got slandered for my attempts to make her feel beautiful.

It hurts to know that she'll never know how beautiful she is. Her mirror is a goddamn liar, and deserves to be thrown deep in the pits of Tartarus. I wish she saw herself like I saw her. She shined brighter than the brightest star. Maybe that's why the night sky full of stars reminded me of her. Maybe someday she'll know her worth, and feel beautiful.

Thanks to my bloody saviour complex, I wanted to save her from her sorrow. I wanted her to be happy. I didn't know how to make her, but I would never stop trying.

"Can I see your scars?"

She looked down, and came sat next to me. I glanced upon her arms, and legs.

Beautiful scars on critical veins.

"Please stop. Please don't do it again. Don't hurt yourself. You're too perfect to feel this way. Promise me you won't do it again."

She just shook her head. I held her hand.

> *The deeper you cut, the deeper I hurt.*
> *The deeper you cut, it only gets worse.*

She thanked me for the beautiful lyric. I told her to call me whenever she felt this way. She told me to stop being a hypocrite.

Oh, that's right! She knows your secret.
It's okay, she told me hers. It's only fair I tell her how I really feel.
You're giving yourself too much importance. You're worthless, you know?
I know. Please leave for now.

Then, we talked about how the sad gets worse at night, and it gets so hard to battle that it feels like we lost the war.

"I love you so much,"
I said, as I watched her fall asleep.

I looked at her house, again, and then walked back to Digboi's place.

I knocked on his window, and he opened it, and let me in.

"What the hell, dude? It's freaking 4 a.m.!"

I apologized, and hugged him so much that he had to forgive me for waking him up so early.

My mom picked me up, in the morning.
I hugged Digboi, and thanked his mom for having me over.

A NEW WEEK TALEN

I studied my butt off for the half-yearly examinations.

I studied a lot.

Emphasis on the 'a lot'.

I spent five days studying for Biology, mainly due to the fact that our Biology teacher gave us a butt load of notes to study from. So, I had to memorize sixteen features of every phylum in Animalia and Plant kingdom, and it consumed a lot of time. Then, I also had to memorize the name of every tissue in the human body, which was a downright inhumane task for someone with a horrible memory like me.

The other time, I studied math. I studied it so much. I needed an A+, in every subject, to finally get a 4.0 GPA. I was pretty sure I wouldn't get an A in French, though. I found French very hard.

So, I would have studied about 125 hours in total, and the outcome was disastrous.

No freaking thing came from the Animalia and Plant Kingdom - Phylum crap, and all that came was weird generic shit that we weren't even taught, like 'What is an incubation period?'

I messed it up, again.

After three days of acute piles (it's not my fault, it's hereditary), I had to go to school, as we were to get the results.

If it were up to me, I would take with me a hand grenade, and blow the school up to pieces.

I took a shower, drank three glasses of water (apparently, it helps in preventing piles), dried my hair, wore my NUKETOWN 2025 tee, and a purple shirt over it, and then tightened my shoelaces, and went to school.

There, I'd get depressed again.

Ken thug-hugged me, and he sat next to me.

K: "What up, my man?"
A: "I'm fine, thank you, Ken."
K: "Okay, man."
A: "Hm."
K: "So, you bang Thea yet?"
A: "What? No, I do not want to bang her."
K: "Haha. Sure thing."
A: "I just want to get over her."

K: "You mean you want to get OVER her."
A: "Oh my god. Stop, Ken."

Ken's sense of humor got out of control, sometimes.

~~~~~~

Shortly, we got the results.
Here's what I got.

My overall grade came out to be A-.

So, naturally, I wanted to cry.

I felt so disappointing again.

I know. Such a petty thing to get depressed over. What a loser. So I got a bunch of Bs and Cs. What's the big deal?

I'll explain.

I want to become a physicist when I grow up.

For that, you need to go to a good college.

For that, you need to have a 4.0 GPA.

For that, you need to get all A+s.

In other words, I messed up my future.

So, yes, I was sad.

Well, sadder than usual.

Let me get this straight. My mom and dad aren't bad parents. I'm not saying that because they don't beat on me, or physically, or sexually abuse me. I'm saying this because they actually are amazing parents, with just tad high expectations.

It kills me to disappoint them, with everything that I do.

The feeling of being a disappointment to my parents aggravates my depression.

And my grades aggravate the feeling of being a disappointment.

Sitting on my seat, with my head down, I wished I knew how to hide my feelings.

I wanted to hide my feelings, so my friends wouldn't come over, next to me, every two minutes, and ask me what was wrong, or that it was okay to get the grades I got.

I didn't want them to do that, because I didn't want them to pity me, and partly because they didn't understand what getting good grades meant to me.

Mostly, nobody understood why I was so sad over getting decent grades like mine, because they did not have expectations as high as mine, and nor did their parents.

Now, Sidnee, who is most obviously a genius, got all As, and they perfectly complemented her perfect 4.0 GPA. Sometimes I imagine how proud her parents must be, of her. Honest, I felt jealous of how perfectly smart and smartly perfect Sidnee was.

Digboi performed even worse than I did, but he didn't care much. He was talented at many other things, and his father had a well established business so eve if he didn't get a good job, he had something to fall back upon.

I was really sad.
I really was sad.

I wondered how disappointed mom and dad would be, when I'd go back home and tell them my grades.

Allen patted my back, and said,
"Well, Adam, you know, your parents won't disown you."

A: "I know. They should've done that when I was two."

Al: "They wouldn't."

A: "They should have."

Al: "Why?"

A: "I don't deserve such good people. They're terribly ill-fortuned."

Allen was one of those people I could tell anything to.

Three weeks ago, I had a dream about the dead guy.

It brought back my sorrow.

I thought about how thwarted I was, and how messed up.

I really did mess everything up.

I made everyone who ever talked to me, or cared about me, feel like shit. And that made me feel like shit.

Damn, Newton was right, even non-physically.

It was easier for Newton and the other guys. They had so much stuff to discover, that it was easy for them to be successful.

Here and now, 90% of all phenomenon have already been discovered and nothing is left for me to do. Ugh.

Allen said to me,
"Adam, your parents are not disappointed in you."

A: "They are."
Al: "No, they are not. You just think they are. Or, you want to think that they are, when really, it's you that is disappointed in yourself, and you just want to hide the fact."

Allen could have been right, but he probably wasn't.

A: "No, they are."
Al: "Did they tell you that?"
A: "Not directly."
Al: "So, how?"
A: "I just… it's… it's very hard to explain… I just… the look in their eyes says it."
Al: "Go home and ask them if they're disappointed in you. And tell me what they say."
A: "Okay."
Al: "Oh, and Adam…"
A: "Yes?"

Allen tore out a page from the back of his notebook, and wrote down three numbers.

Al: "Adam, the next time you feel like killing yourself, call me. I'll surely pick up any one of these three."
A: "Okay."
Al: "Seriously. Don't die. I'll punch you really hard, if you do."
A: "Okay."
Al: "There's a very, very small chance that I won't pick any of the three up. Still, call me anytime you feel like dying."
A: "I'll have to call you each second of each day, then."
Al: "Any. Time."
A: "Thank you, Allen."

I went back home, and I told my results to my mom. Like I had anticipated, she was highly disappointed in me.

She gave me a lecture on how I was screwing up my future, and how hard it is to get into a good college, and get a good job. She also told me to stop making that sad, little, pathetic, depressed face, and to stop crying over spilt milk.

I couldn't take it any longer. I really couldn't.

FEBRUARY 18

I couldn't sleep the whole night. I just couldn't.

I thought about Thea, the whole time.

My eyes hurt, and I wanted to cry, just let it all out, but I couldn't.

I just wanted it all to end.

Will I still go to heaven, if I kill myself?

And the worst part of it all was that I don't even believe in God.

All I believed in was *Genocide*.

I looked myself inside my room, and started punching the walls, after waking up.

It was about seven on the clock.

Part of me wanted to call Allen, and talk it through.

The other part of me wanted to write a note, and slit my throat.

Suicide seems so tempting.

Look through my eyes and you decide if I'm a human being,
My soul was ripped from me.

I never would have gone, but I had nothing else to do, so, when Digboi called me up, and asked if I'd like to chill with him and flirt with girls at Starbucks, I said yes.

I also got a call from Sidnee, asking if I wanted to go for a Chelsea Grin concert.
I really like Chelsea Grin, but I hate crowds, and there are no concerts without crowds.

I was unwilling to go, but he told me that Thea was coming, too.

So, I apologized to Digboi, and asked my dad to drop me off at the concert, and there, Sidnee handed me a ticket, and we went inside.

Take me away.
I'll go down to the depths of this nightmare made real.

The concert was amazing. They played Recreant, My Damnation, and The Foolish One, and they played astonishingly well. They took a little break, and Sidnee waved at me, and told me to go talk to Thea.

So, I went, and stood next to Thea. I didn't say anything, however. I just stood, next to her, staring in awe, at her beauty.

It killed me to be this close to her, and still be so far away.

Take me away from this.

I still couldn't talk to her, so we awkwardly stared at the band, each member drinking water, and revisiting lyrics for the next song.

I remembered the first time I heard Thea sing. It was during class, and she was humming.

Thea sang like an angel, as well as, smelt like one. (I should use her shampoo.)

I wanted to just talk to her, endlessly, but Chelsea Grin started performing again, and of course, it was something that you just cannot miss.

The guitar riffs were amazing.

insert a lot of head banging

Thea looked at me, and then she looked away.

I looked at her, and maybe she knew that, but I kept looking, anyway.

The guy next to me dropped his hot dog, and exclaimed,
"Oh, shit! My wiener!"

This is why I hated crowds. Someone said something stupid, and in the end, someone almost got hurt. So, I kept my mouth shut, and looked at the amazing band perform.

After the concert was over, all of us got donuts, and Sidnee left Thea and I alone.

I said,
"I absolutely love donuts."
"No shit,"
said Thea.

I waited for a moment, and said,
"Well, donuts make me feel better. They reduce my tendency to kill myself."

T: "YES. It's the same thing with me, with M&Ms."
A: "I'll get you some M&Ms, then."
T: "No, don't do that. I already had a lot in the morning."
A: "Hm. Okay."
T: "Uh huh."
A: "I just wish I could afford anti-depressants."
T: "Maybe we could buy it together?"
A: "Yes, that'd be great. I'll sell my kidneys, and then we can go buy anti-depressants."
T: "Okay." (I was hoping that she'd laugh on that pathetic attempt to a joke, but she didn't. Such a pity.)
A: "Okay."

About half an hour later, my mom picked me up, and I said goodbye to my friends.

Mom: "How was the concert?"
A: "It was amazing!"
Mom: "Did you have fun?"
A: "Yes, a lot."
Mom: "That's really nice, Adam."
A: "Thanks. I love you, Mom."

Back home, I ate dinner, and then I slept at nine thirty, because my mom asked me to.

I dreamt about weird dudes singing and playing the guitar, and then my conversation with Thea, all night long.

Well, not all night long, because I got a call, in the middle of the night.

I pulled my phone from underneath my pillow, and I answered the call, from an unknown number.

"Hey."
"Hey."
"Adam?"
"Yes, hi."
"It's Thea."

Were my dreams coming true?

    A: "Oh, hey."
    T: "Hi."
    A: "Hey."
    T: "How are you?"
    A: "How do you think I am? How are you, Thea?"
    T: "I think you're okay. I'm okay. Everything's okay. How can everything be okay?"

Yes, everything was okay. I don't know how everything was okay.

    A: "I love you, Thea."
    T: "Come outside. I'm outside your house."
    A: "Hm. What?"

T: "Come outside."
A: "Okay."

I stared out of my window, and I saw a beautiful silhouette.

She hung up, I grabbed my jacket, and then I snuck out of my window.

I could have used the front door, too, and even if my parents had woken up, they wouldn't scold me, much. But still, I didn't want to wake them up, so I snuck out of my window.

I walked towards that beautiful silhouette, and slowly, the beautiful silhouette turned into the girl I adored.

I stared at her, rubbing my eyes, and she didn't seem to mind.

T: "Let's go buy anti-depressants."
A: "Okay."
T: "Let's go, Adam."

Thea looked really pretty, even at midnight. Then, I realized, that I didn't have any money with me.

A: "I don't have any money."
T: "That's okay. I do."

I still had so many questions.

First, I wondered if it was just a dream. It was highly improbable that Thea would come outside my house, that too, at the middle of the night.

Second, had she started to like me, too? That'd be even more improbable to occur.

> A: "How'd you know my address?"
> T: "Sidnee."
> A: "Ah, okay."

I looked around, and I didn't see any car, or bike, or cycle.

It was just she, and I, in the dead of the night.

Nearly dead.

> A: "How'd you come here?"
> T: "My sister dropped me. She was driving to a party, and it was hardly a detour."
> A: "Oh, okay."
> T: "Any more questions?"

Yes.

> A: "Why me?"
> T: "I want to love you, Adam."

I didn't reply for a while.
I stared blankly, in awe.

Then, I said,

"Can we hold hands?"
"Sure."

I grabbed her hand, and held it tight.

It was warm.

It was nice.

It was nice, pretending that she was mine.

It was nice.

—————————————————————

Thea checked her phone, for the nearest pharmacy, where they sold anti-depressants.

It was three miles away, and she was looking for the way there, but I told her that I knew the way. She said okay, and then shivered. I took off my jacket, and put it on her, and she wore it.

"Thank you."
"Always."

—————————————————————

We walked for a mile, or so, when Thea looked at me, and said,
"How often do you think about suicide? You don't need to answer."

I didn't feel like lying to Thea. The end was so close, anyway.

The end to all our problems.

Either way.

"I believe the question is how often do I not think about suicide. And the answer is, never. I never think about anything other than suicide."

She shook her head. She nodded her head. She did it at the same time.

She did that quite a lot.

And yes, she looked adorable, when she did it.

We walked another fifteen meters, when she replied,
"So, Adam, any non-suicidal girls, lately?"

I smiled, and said,
"No, just the one."

    T: "One non-suicidal girl?"
    A: "No, just the one suicidal girl."
    T: "Oh."

A: "Just the one pretty little suicidal girl."

She smiled, and I hoped she really meant it.

We turned left, at the diversion, and there, we saw the pharmacy.

"We're here."
Thea held my hand tighter, and that's when I realized that we had been holding hands ever since I asked her if we could. It felt so nice.

I felt like I could be saved.

I felt like the problems were going to end.

Thea pulled my sleeve, gently, and we entered the pharmacy.

She knocked on the table, and asked the chemist, "Do you have any anti-depressants?"

The chemist, who was scratching his goatee, said, "Yeah, but wouldn't you prefer to buy condoms?"

Thea looked at me, and her eyes told me to let her take over the situation.
"Just tell me. How much for anti-depressants?"

The chemist, who now, I doubt, actually was a chemist, snorted, and said,
"Forty bucks."

Thea looked at me, and whispered,
"Shit. I have only thirty. Do you have any money?"

I searched my pockets, and I found a crumpled five-dollar bill.

"Yeah, I have five bucks."
"Shit."

She asked the chemist if he'd give her a discount, but he wouldn't.

Thea returned from the counter, and looked at me.

I looked into her eyes.

I could look, forever.

But she didn't believe in forever, and I wasn't sure, if I did, too.

Her eyes watered, and a tear fell down.

Tears don't fall, they just crash around me.

Then it hit me.

It wasn't that we couldn't afford the anti-depressants that made her cry.

It was the bigger picture.

Her scars. Her suicidal self. Something horrible had happened.

And no, the problems were not going away.

Even if we had gotten the anti-depressants, the problems would still have been there.

I hadn't really known Thea very well.
I hadn't really known her for long.
But I understood how she felt.
It hurt me.
It hurt her.
It hurt us.

Everything hurt.

We had no reason.
We had no purpose.
Just a worthless boy and a disoriented girl.

It all would go on.
And I didn't want it to.

I really didn't.

Life will go on, forever.
Life will go on, ~~forever~~.
~~Life~~ will go on, ~~forever~~.
~~Life will~~ go ~~on~~, ~~forever~~.

Before leaving the pharmacy, I handed the five-dollar bill to the most-probably-an-uncertified-chemist, and bought a Vitamin-D capsule. Also, before we left, I said,
"Keep the change, you filthy animal."

Thea high-fived me for that, and laughed.

"What do we do now?"
Thea asked me, wiping her tears.

I regret this so heavily, but I said,
"I have cyanide…"

She stared at me, and whispered,
        "Really?"

I could have lied. I should have lied.

I really should have.

But I didn't, and that's what changed everything.

I stared back into her sad eyes, and said,
        "Yes."

I had picked that bottle of cyanide on the day I had seen the dead guy. And then, I put it in my pocket, so that Ken couldn't see. I had hidden it in my drawer, as soon as I got in my room.

She held my hand, and it warmed me up, inside.

"Adam, let's go to your room."

I nodded, and we walked towards my house in the dead of night.

She jumped inside my room through the window, then, so did I.

She waited, peacefully, as I searched for cyanide.

I found it under my notebooks.

I picked it up, and then Thea held my hand again. We jumped out, together.

Thea looked at me, and I looked at her, and after three minutes of us staring at each other, and then at the cyanide bottle, I said,

"I just wanted to save you."

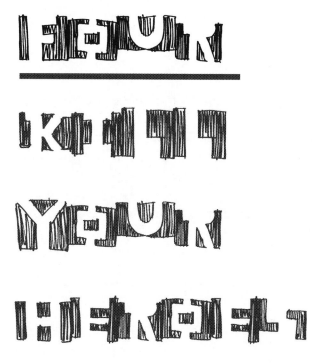

"I just wanted to save you."

She looked into my eyes, and the look absolutely killed me. Well, not literally, yet.

Then, she said,
"Save me? Like I'm some lost puppy?"

I shook my head, and I said softly,
"I just wish you could she the way I see you. How perfect you are."

She smiled, but then, her smiled faded away, and she replied,
"I guess some things cannot be saved."

***

Thea held my hand, again, and looked up at the stars.

I looked up, at the stars, too.

They looked beautiful.

The stars looked beautiful.

This night is flawless, don't you let it go.

***

Thea came closer, and I held her tight.
She held me tighter.

I'm wonderstruck, dancing around all alone.

She smiled, and asked me if I was ready.

I'll spend forever wondering if you knew.

I nodded, and took out two pills from the cyanide bottle, and Thea smiled, as I did.

I was enchanted to meet you.

When she looked up at the stars, again, I threw away one pill from my hand, and took out the Vitamin-D capsule from my pocket.

Thea said,
"You're my hero, Adam."

I smiled,
"Kill you heroes, Thea. They are worthless."

Thea said,
"Cheers to escaping this messed up life."

We were still hugging each other, but we let go, and I handed her the capsule.

"On three, okay?"
"Okay."

I smiled.

"One."

I held the pill, tightly.

"Two."
I opened my mouth.

"Three."

I put the pill inside, and swallowed it.

Thea had taken up the capsule, too. She smiled, and said,
"I bet they won't even notice that I'm gone, until they find me dead in the evening, when mom asks me to walk the dog."

I held her face, and said,
"I would."

She smiled, and said,
"I know."

We held each other, again.

"Thea, promise me, if you survive, you'll take it as a sign from the universe, and try being happy. Stop hurting yourself. Try to stop the hurt. Stay alive, then, okay? Promise me."

Reluctancy, followed by a moment of glimpsing into each other's eyes. The darkness of our souls went through the pupils, and we looked into our true selves.

"I promise."

~~~~~~

We looked up, at the stars, again.

After about thirteen minutes, Thea's sister called her, and asked her to meet her on the diversion.

I walked Thea till the diversion, and she held me, the tightest, tonight.

I was glad I could save her.

~~~~~~

As she drove away, I wondered what impact my death would cause.

My parents would wonder why I wouldn't wake up, tomorrow. Hopefully, they'd see my unfinished book, with every encounter with depression that I had. Hopefully, they'd forgive me.

Sidnee and Digboi would wonder why I didn't come to school. Digboi would call my cellphone, and he wouldn't get through. Sidnee and Digboi would wonder why I didn't come to school for an entire week. Sidnee would call me, too, and she wouldn't get through. Then, she'd call my mom's number, and get an invitation to my funeral. Hopefully, they'd forgive me.

Ken would try to tell himself that it's all a joke, and then, bang his head against the wall, and then, Andrea. He'd probably be pissed at me.

Allen would be sad, and he'd tell his psychiatrist about every conversation he had with me. Hopefully, he'd forgive me.

Thea would hate me. Hopefully, she'd forget me. Hopefully, she'd keep our promise.

I hadn't left a suicide note, because I didn't need to.

Why have an ending to a story that doesn't even matter?

I wanted to just go home, and sneak in, through my window, and sleep.

And never wake up.

Then, as I walked on the empty road, I saw headlights, brighter every second.

As I stared, and tried to make sense of what was happening, the headlights became brighter.

A black Chevrolet Impala ran me over.

A NOTE FROM LIFE WANNABE

This book does NOT promote self-harm, cutting, poisoning, self-defamation, self-pity, depression, or suicide in any way. This is merely a platform for me to get across my words to a large audience, and I hope it doesn't influence anybody.

More importantly, I endorse getting help if you're sad. Talk to somebody you love. Talk to somebody who loves you. Talk to your parents, I'm sure they'll understand. If not, talk to your friends. If you need a friend, I'm here for you. If it starts getting out of hand, see a psychologist. If you can't afford/ trust one, then I'm here (not sure if I'm as useful, though).

Stay alive. You're beautiful. Please stay alive. Stay alive for me. None of that 'stick around for your family' bullshit. I mean, that's important, but you must increase your self-worth. I know that's hard to do. But it gets better. I promise, it really does. Stick around for that. New pop-punk music comes out every day! New badass movies release! New Kate Upton photo shoots! Making out! *beep*! More lame ass books by me!

Hold on, kid. This ride's a wild one.

ACKNOWLEDGEMENTS

There are so many people that I would give my utmost thanks to (this seems grammatically incorrect, I don't know).

The following people are very important to me, and I would give them all Nobel Peace Prizes if it were upto me.

EDITOR CLUB

The first adult who read my novel, and didn't declare me insane. Thank you for showing me what to do after the writing process. I know I'm annoying, but it cannot be helped.

MY PARENTS

for not giving up on me. If this becomes a bestseller, I'll buy you a Lamborghini Veneno Roadster (just kidding, I'll just get you a new bicycle).

MY SISTER

for being such a cutie. You're kawaii, and I adore you.

JACKIE ELONGHI

for knowing me like the back of your hand.

KARLA KITH

for the good times, bromance, and dark jokes. Good luck with whatever lies ahead.

BRYAN MUKHERJEE

for Eternal Subside, not giving up, and for beating your sadness. I'm proud of you for staying. #stayaliveclique

LARA MENDE

for being an unscrupulous super major bitch, and for the advice, the emails and the encouragement, and oh, so much else.

THANKING "MARK" LANYAN

just because you wanted me to mention your name here. I love you; we should chill.

THE BANDS THAT SAVED MY LIFE

You'll probably see a lot of lyrics in this book. That's because music is such an important part of my life.

I would like to give credit to all the following artists for continuously inspiring me, and saving oh, so many lives other than mine.

blink-182
All Time Low
AWOLNATION
New Found Glory
My Chemical Romance
A Day To Remember
Chelsea Grin
Bring Me The Horizon
Twenty One Pilots
La Dispute

…and the list goes on and on and on. Check out my Tumblr for more amazing bands to listen to.

THANK YOU

for buying this crappy book. Do write to me to tell me if you like it. I promise I'll reply as soon as I get the modem back from my dad.

XOXO

ABOUT THE AUTHOR

AKSHAT THAKUR
is a wannabe writer,
influenced by real
writers such as Ned
Vizzini, John Green,
and Stephen Chbosky.
He likes punk rock and
anime, and he wants to
build a rocketship and
fly far away. You might
find him in his boxers

and bathrobe, trying to re-enact that scene
from Fight Club, or hanging with his best
friend Ricky Khandelwal.

You should write to him, if you want to vent,
or if you're sad, or happy, free, confused and
lonely at the same time, at
AKSHAT.CONNECTIN@GMAIL.COM.

You should also follow him on Tumblr, he's got a rad blog.
URNOTEVENPUNKROCK.TUMBLR.COM
(This might change in a few months, unless he's Tumblr famous)